AN
Angel's
JOURNEY

RUSSELL J. CLARK

iUniverse, Inc.
Bloomington

An Angel's Journey

This is a work of fiction. All of the characters, names, incidents, organizations, and dialogue in this novel are either the products of the author's imagination or are used fictitiously.

iUniverse books may be ordered through booksellers or by contacting:

iUniverse
1663 Liberty Drive
Bloomington, IN 47403
www.iuniverse.com
1-800-Authors (1-800-288-4677)

Because of the dynamic nature of the Internet, any web addresses or links contained in this book may have changed since publication and may no longer be valid. The views expressed in this work are solely those of the author and do not necessarily reflect the views of the publisher, and the publisher hereby disclaims any responsibility for them.

Any people depicted in stock imagery provided by Thinkstock are models, and such images are being used for illustrative purposes only.
Certain stock imagery © Thinkstock.

ISBN: 978-1-4759-5870-6 (sc)
ISBN: 978-1-4759-5868-3 (hc)
ISBN: 978-1-4759-5869-0 (ebk)

Printed in the United States of America

iUniverse rev. date: 11/12/2012

AN
Angel's
JOURNEY

To my mom, who taught me love by loving me unconditionally. Without this teaching and this love, I might have been lost and unable find my way in the emotional abyss of the *journey*.

To my teachers at Ithaca High School, Mrs. Anne Emory, Mr. John Clark, and Mr. Byron Rempp, who cared about me and taught me science, culture, and history while opening my mind and challenging me. The wisdom of their influence has traveled with me throughout my journey.

CONTENTS

INTRODUCTION

It was a warm, balmy spring day on the beach on Florida's Treasure Coast. My wife and children were on spring break from school—she from teaching and they from studying. So, as the tradition went, I took a week of vacation and we made the arduous trek by car from the cold gray of a Michigan March to the sun, the warmth, and Grandpa and Grandma. We all endured the miles. My wife and I endured the same questions asked thousands of times: "Are we there yet?" "I've got to go potty. Can we stop?" and "I'm hungry. Can we eat now?"

I lay on my towel in the warm sand. The trip down was all but forgotten. By 12:30 in the afternoon, I was thoroughly intoxicated by the sun, warm sand, ocean, and peaceful, warm breeze. Inevitably, I dozed off.

In a flash of light, I entered a tunnel and began to dream. Papoo came to me and told me a story. He told me it was an important story and I should write it down for others to read. He said if I did write it down, it could even help others on their journeys. In the dream, the story was so clear, the lessons so obviously true and in need of saying, that of course I promised to write it down.

Hours later, it seemed, I fell out of the tunnel. I realized that I had been asleep for thirty minutes, and I lay in the sun a few more minutes while contemplating the dream. I didn't know whether to be amused by my imagination, sobered by inspiration, or awed by my own silliness. I did not get up and start writing it down, nor did I tell anyone. Certainly, a promise made in a dream is not a real commitment. Or is it?

In the years that followed, Papoo continued to visit me in my dreams. He added to the story, and I wondered at my unconscious creativity, even finding it somewhat humorous. It was when Papoo began to invade my waking moments that I began to think seriously about writing the story down. I also contemplated my own sanity. *Perhaps I should seek serious counseling or check into a hotel with padded cells?* I also asked myself, *Would a shrink ask me any questions that I had not already asked myself? Would I have any better answers for a stranger than I do for myself?*

So . . . I am writing it down to purge myself of the need to do so and perhaps help some other traveler as a result. I have forgotten some of the more complex details of the story—or should I say *stories?*—that Papoo told me. Perhaps I never brought them with me out of the tunnel. The whole experience is a bit like going to class and understanding the lecture perfectly while in the classroom but then forgetting some of it upon leaving. Since Papoo does not report at my beck and call, I will do the best I can. As the story goes, I am now willing.

This is how the story came to me. It is a work of fiction. It is not meant to be science fiction, nor is it a theological treatise. It is a story. It might be a parable. I have employed certain unconventional and creative devices, such as cryptic spelling and invented words and phrases that came to me as I wrote. For example, I believe that you will quickly and easily realize that the Eternal Continuum of Perfection is heaven, that Firterra is earth, and that the words are conveying something about the concept as well as the place. I have not explicitly connected all of the dots for you because they did not come to me connected. I know how they connect for me, and I think you will find your own connections as well.

RJC

CHAPTER 1

OVERTURE: BEFORE THE JOURNEY

At Work in the Eternal Continuum of Perfection

Papoo sat in his office, contemplating how to assist these beings entering the Trakis II event horizon. As the natural law arbitrator for Universe Delta III, it was his responsibility to protect intelligent life-forms from disasters. He analyzed complex situations and all of the various forces at work and implemented solutions that assisted the life-forms from Firterra in achieving the Creator's purpose. All this had to be done without breaking any of the natural laws. One of Papoo's special abilities was a real-time conscious awareness of thoughts of these creatures. He also sensed their feelings—or perhaps more correctly, the effects of their feelings—on their behavior. He was not omniscient, nor was he omnipresent. Those were qualities of the Creator. These life-forms were special. They were made in the Creator's image and possessed a burning desire for learning and adventure, which many of them pursued with all the energy of their lives. These beings also possessed freedom of choice connected with their infinite essence. It was this gift of free moral agency for which Papoo longed. He swore that if his chance ever came for that great test and adventure, he would not forget the objective, the reward, or who he really was. Papoo and his best friend, Xoderap, often discussed the challenges and dangers, as best they knew, of the voluntary missions and assignments. Both were interested in serving the Creator's purpose wherever they could help the most.

Papoo was aware that others had taken assignments and not accomplished their objectives. Some had never found their purpose. Still others had chosen, in three dimensions, not to pursue the objectives or accept the missions previously agreed to. In addition, he was eager to respond to the Creator's call for volunteers to confront the developing crisis on Firterra.

The arbitrator smiled as he realized the solution to the problem approaching Trakis II. As was so often the case, the transportation device was not properly configured to withstand the force fields set up by a first-class creation known to them as a black hole. The developer, or black hole, was a truly marvelous system capable of totally reconstituting the time-space continuum. This particular developer, Trakis II, was a wonderful device into which and out of which several galaxies had already disappeared and been spawned from. More than one group of travelers had been flung into different time spaces and environments by the slingshot maneuver from Trakis II.

Papoo was not always able to manage the events as he wished. Sometimes, things happened quite beyond even *his* ability to influence or change. Then life journeys really got botched up. Imagine going on a routine visit to the next galaxy—just visiting or on business—and ending up in an era before your grandmother without knowing that time is just a limiting dimension. Papoo watched as the adventuring ship approached Trakis II and the ship's control center went berserk. The electronic controls were completely useless when confronted by an energy absorber so powerful that even light was absorbed by it. This was a most difficult concept for these creatures with their perception of their own inherent, but not inevitable, physical design limitations. The ship was nearing the point of no return. The travelers were terrorized by the innumerable inputs assaulting their real essence. They were unable to verbalize what seemed to be real and what they were sure was reality. The ship was accelerating toward a fateful rendezvous when . . .

The arbitrator grasped the opportunity, the moment, as the giant and unseen Trakis II hurled the ship far into the galaxy Crkon. Papoo smiled again as he observed the travelers admiring their perceptions of their younger physical bodies. *Oh well*, he thought. *They have already discovered the way that little trick works. I hope they figure out where they are soon.*

Papoo was the originator of the black hole escape formula, using a ship's own trajectory to move it close to the event horizon and then using the acceleration force from the black hole to escape again. The Omniscient One had simply smiled when Papoo was invited to demonstrate the maneuver. Papoo realized how simple the concept really was. He was considered very intelligent and quite creative in his own group.

Papoo had first gained special attention from the Omniscient One when he formally requested a Life-Event assignment through his sector overseer, the renowned Gabriel. Few could understand how an arbitrator could wish to leave his perfection for such a risky, although exciting and potentially rewarding, adventure. Gabriel understood. He had survived the great test in the old way, but many friends, including his best friend, had not.

Lucifer, Michael, Raphael, Melchizedek, and Gabriel had been very close to each other and to the Creator. They were a part of the Creator's early and little understood work and formed His inner circle. No other beings created after them possessed either their perception or their creative abilities.

Michael was always the wise one. He was one of the great communicators sent by the Creator to some of His living work. Lucifer always seemed to be obsessed with competing with his peers, and indeed with the Omniscient One. It started out with simple cosmic games. Later, Lucifer actually challenged the Creator for the position of Supreme Being. In spite of Michael's and Gabriel's reasoning and pleading, he persisted in the challenge. Gabriel reasoned that the Creator had not been elected or invited to the position of Supreme Being. He simply *was* and *is*. Many times these friends met throughout the cosmos and in newly created universes to discuss the origin of the Creator.

The five archangels searched around the cosmos for other beings and tested the Creator's omniscience by asking Him about their journeys. His replies were perfect descriptions of places, events, and discussions. Even this Lucifer questioned. "He knows our thoughts, but He may not really be omniscient," he declared to Gabriel. Gabriel's love for Lucifer was strong, and he reasoned that the Omniscient One, the Creator, had created them and not they Him; therefore, Lucifer's challenge was totally unfounded. Perhaps it was the simplicity of the logic or the perfection of the proofs, or perhaps it was the fact of the Creator's nearly complete silence when he was pressed to explain His origin. He responded with a benevolent smile and only the statement "I am," which frustrated Lucifer. Gabriel demanded that Lucifer "consider the absolute perfection of the Creator and be careful not to break the laws of behavior, lest the consequences prescribed by the Creator be set in motion. Remember the penalties are an inevitable part of creation! The Creator's love for you as His most brilliant and beautiful creation will not be enough to save even you!" Lucifer paused to consider and left the presence of his friend. There were many changes in the continuum after that meeting.

When Lucifer returned from his thoughts and wanderings, he was strikingly changed. He had lost his lightness. His aura was dark and somber, and his communication was morbid and unreasonable. He no longer seemed capable of the great love that he had been so famous for creatively expressing.

Gabriel reminded Lucifer that there were consequences for competing, contradicting, or disobeying the Creator, but he lost the argument with Lucifer and often grieved for his friend. Sometimes, they ran into each other and even fought when Gabriel was on assignments. He was still an awesome creature, once brilliant and fascinating but now dark and evil. A totally loveless creature he had become. Gabriel warned Papoo, "Beware of Lucifer on your journey, for he will be aware of you and will be looking for ways to distract you from your purpose."

Gabriel and Papoo often discussed the joys and dangers of a Life-Event assignment. Papoo dreamed of surviving the assignment and returning home with an understanding of the Creator. *After all, he would muse to himself, how difficult can it be to travel to another dimension and existence and simply retain a remembrance of this dimension and the transformation to three dimensions and the assignment, as it was known to some?* Throughout the assignment, he would retain his own personal essence, that unique omnidimensional quality that was the basis for his being.

Gabriel warned, "It is not as you think. You may lose all memory of your present existence. Furthermore, you may not even remember your other dimensions. The journey is long and difficult. You may retain some memory of this existence. You can do great good, but the evil you can do on this journey is also very great. At the location you have requested, the dark forces exerted on you will be extremely great. Your potential loss of memory on the journey puts you at grave risk. Lucifer will know of you. As you know, his forces are very vigilant in their attention to the comings and goings from our section of the continuum. The dark forces exerted by Lucifer will be cleverly disguised. The clarity of your perception of reality will be impacted by a multitude of distractions and stimuli that you have never before experienced. Nor have I. My test was very different. When Lucifer rebelled, we all had a choice to accept, love, and obey the Creator or to challenge Him and join Lucifer in his challenge to the Creator. It was easy for me to choose the one who had created me. I had not really thought much about what being exiled from the Eternal Continuum of Perfection looked like, and I was shocked and horrified by how awful it is."

Papoo occupied much of his existence trying to understand his assignment and test and the forces of the journey. He simply could not understand why there should be a loss of knowledge, multidimensional perception, and memory in the lower dimensional transition process. How could he lose his memory of prior existence? It was all a part of his essence, wasn't it?

He understood well the limitations that a three-dimensional body represented. What baffled him were the limitations that seemed to be projected to the beings' essence. Some the beings on Firterra actually didn't believe in their own essence. Some believed that essence or the soul was acquired at death and was either rewarded or punished based on the life of the being to which it was abstractly attached. As Papoo studied the destination of his assignment, he was sometimes convinced that Gabriel was incorrect in his descriptions of the difficulty of remembering the assignment and the purpose of the journey. How could the journey and the transformation impact his being to the extent that he could not remember what he now knew? Further thoughts of the test, Lucifer, and his dream only perplexed him.

Papoo concentrated on his job to quell the yearning that was swelling in his being for a greater challenge. Gabriel was a source of encouragement as Papoo attempted to gain an audience with the Creator, and Gabriel continued his council on the hazards of the journey.

Two Archangels' Views of the Journey

At a particularly long and strenuous session during their travels, Gabriel said to Papoo, "Don't you understand that just the transformation and travel itself is dangerous? Once the transformation is completed, the journey begins. We can provide little protection for you there. You will be subjected to a vast array of sensory inputs, which you can only absorb. You will not immediately be able to comprehend all of the stimuli, but it will all be saved for future integration and processing as you are able. You will not be able to communicate with either dimension on the journey.

"Once you arrive at your assignment, you will be very vulnerable to feelings, which you have never experienced. You may not have a memory of this present state to use as a frame of reference. Well ... you *will* have a memory, but it may fade out or it may be taught and programmed over. I can see that you doubt me! Pause to consider the several travelers that you have known and loved who have gone on assignments since your creation. Can you think of one that you would have recognized our connection with, in the 3-D state, without already knowing? No! Not one! You will probably think that you are alone and the attacks from the dark side will be vicious. Lucifer will recognize you for what you have been as well as who you are, just as I will. At times when you can remember this existence and think of it, you may be told it is a fantasy ... that it just isn't possible, or perhaps you are crazy. You must stand firm in your beliefs and carry out your mission. We can help you, but you will have to believe and ask for help."

"But ..." Papoo protested, *"I do believe, and I will ask for help."*

"It's not the same now," Gabriel continued. "You must believe and ask for help when you are there. It sounds very easy and simple now. There you will be taught to be self-reliant and strong within the confines of three dimensions. The dark side will tell you that the influence and power of the light side does not exist. You may even come to believe that there is no other dimension, or as they would say, no supernatural. We will be there to help, but you must ask. You will seek and be taught knowledge and wisdom through logical paradigms. Remember there will be many illusions. The Wise One, Solomon, wrote concerning the pursuit of knowledge and wisdom in three-dimensional existence that with much wisdom comes much sorrow and the more knowledge, the more grief.

You will read, or perhaps be taught, what seem to be paradoxes that exhort you to be or act in ways that seem rather stupid and contradictory to the logical flow of life in that dimension. You may not know that these are true guides for you. Papoo, I love you. You are at risk! The assignment test is not a game. Failure is fatal, and many have tragically failed. This passionate pursuit of an assignment reminds me of my old friend Lucifer, before he turned to the dark side."

The wise archangel continued. "I will no longer speak in vague terms. You can lose your soul to the dark side. There is a very real chance that if you go to Firterra and fail, you will not gain the prize in the test. Failure is likely forever and too excruciatingly agonizing for even me to contemplate for very long. Many Great Ones have gone before you and failed. In spite of my affection for you, I must tell you that you are a long way from being among the greatest to take the journey and accept the assignment."

Papoo understood well that he was not among the greatest to take the journey and the test. He grasped that there was a chance of failure, but he still felt compelled to go. He replied, "Gabriel, you have taught me and loved me since my creation. You have mentored me. This is something I must do. I must leave this perfection. It bores me because I have not earned it, and I have not chosen it. I have not had an opportunity to be tempted and exercise my will to stay true to the Creator and live and work in the continuum forever. The excitement and anticipation of choosing to be with the Creator after carrying out the assignment brings me joy, and I know it brings the Creator joy as well."

It was clear to Papoo that Gabriel often had memories of the banished Lucifer and several legions of those angels who joined him, and that Gabriel still ached for his lost friend.

Papoo interrupted Gabriel's musing by erupting, "Think of all the good I can do in furthering the Creator's loving purpose for His creations! I must experience the freedom of choice. Free to choose right and be heroic . . . free to make a difference and carry out my mission. Those are things that excite me, and that is why I choose to request a mission. Surely, Gabriel, you remember freedom and choice before you made your critical decision?"

"Freedom!" bellowed Gabriel. "That is a deception even here that most of you do not seem to understand. Freedom is a great irony. If you really understood it, you probably wouldn't want it. It is the embodiment of the assignment you seek. The very concept requires action, foresight, wisdom, and very great responsibility. Few of us in the first creation truly and clearly understood the complete nature of freedom and freewill when we chose to stay with the Creator or join the rebellion. We took our freewill for granted and really did not consider the consequences of choosing to be outside the Creator's purpose. Until the rebellion, we all lived in harmony with the Creator. We had no reason to consider anything but harmony. We all focused on our assignments and pleasing the Creator. We had never observed the consequences of insubordination.

"You are free to ask for the assignment. Once you are on assignment, you are free to reject your mission and go to the dark side. If you enter the second transformation in that state, you will not be free to change your mind. You risk having wasted your freedom for all eternity, and you will not be able to join the Creator ever again."

"But that won't happen to me!" exclaimed Papoo. "I have already told you how much I want to go and carry out my mission, whatever it happens to be."

Gabriel lapsed into a lengthy explanation of the trickery of everyday life on Firterra. He talked of the packaging of good and evil, how evil is often prettied up with apparent good or pleasure but when decisions are irrevocably made and the pretty packaging is stripped away, terrible evils are laid bare. He illustrated how the resolution to do good is frequently most difficult in the stage of choice where the dark outcomes of evil are camouflaged by the appearance of desirability for an initial act. In fact, this deception is not just a cosmetic enhancement but also a downright ingenious deception.

Gabriel spoke in a grave, low-resonant tone that was heavy with all the emotion and love the wise archangel could summon. "The point in the continuum that you will get in your assignment is already known to us who are to be your teachers. The point is that of our old friend's greatest deception. Lucifer will manage to convince millions that he and evil do not exist."

"Oh, surely no one in that dimension or any other would fail to realize and recognize the presence and force of the dark side?" Papoo responded. "Indeed, from what I already know, that would be contrary to much of their science and logic related to the balance of opposites in the universe."

Gabriel responded, "While that is true, you already know that humans often choose to believe what they wish was the truth rather than what is really true."

The discussion that followed lasted for much travel about the universes, and Gabriel illuminated Papoo on the power that wishing to believe exerts over logic, intuition, and even real feelings in the dimension and environment in which he aspired to journey.

Gabriel proceeded. "It will be difficult to choose future happiness and good over present pleasure. Time and the moment play a role in actions in that environment. Throughout your existence, you have not been subject to time. Nor have I. By observation and the tutelage of the Creator, I know that you cannot comprehend the influence of time in an existence that is only three dimensional with your timeless frame of reference. Neither can you now understand that the illusions of life will far overshadow the reality of eternal essence."

Papoo peered quizzically at Gabriel and said, "Are you trying to tell me that I will become confused about time and eternity?"

"No," came the deep, vibrant voice of the archangel. "That is the point. You may not confuse anything. Worse, there will be instances when you will not even pause to consider the relationship of your actions to your ultimate purpose and the consequences of actions and decisions that are of a timeless nature. It is all part of the three-dimensional illusion. As you think about choosing to do right or to carry out your mission, you will think about the impacts, the downside of failure, the obstacles. You may wonder if anyone really cares. You will contemplate all the pleasures you might have missed. You will seldom consider the pain you missed out on if you had made bad choices and abused your freedom. Bad things that happen and the consequences of human actions will often be blamed on the Creator, not the dark side that authors all evil.

"You must try to understand that the beings you will be with. Indeed, you will be one too. They are the inheritors of a predisposed weakness to the dark side. This weakness is a paradox resulting from the curiosity that is an integral part of their creative endowment. They are easily deluded by appearances and are heavily influenced by the limitations of time. Most of them do not view their lives and the existence that they are in as an integral but unique part of a continuum. Rather, they view it as an isolated and discrete event that probably has no connection to another dimension. This explains the influence of time. It is all part of the illusion perpetuated by the dark side. You will witness and hear of many dark events and actions that will astonish you. Lucifer is the great power in that realm. He has been perfecting his craft and has gained much experience. Likewise, the individuals of the human race, which he is attempting to manipulate, and with some success, periodically become more cognizant of their complete and true nature. They grow in spiritual actualization and more of them see through the illusions with increasing frequency. These spiritual awakenings are sometimes turned into excesses by the influence of the Dark One. These periods often end in the persecution of accused witches and warlocks. And this, in turn, causes many sincere thinking people to conclude that this spirituality is, in fact, barbaric and uncivilized. They conclude that no just god would allow some of the behaviors they observe to go on in his behalf. If there is no just god, then it follows that there is no true evil . . . and no Lucifer. That is one great illusion. The planning and manipulation required to successfully implement these illusions are phenomenal. Again, remember these are not beings that evil arises from without encouragement from the dark side. Many do good deeds outside of a mission, but it does not always integrate into the master plan and may not achieve the humanly expected or the desired outcome. They must choose the light and the slipstream to ultimately succeed on their missions. They all are priceless in the next dimensions. They must be encouraged to survive the test."

Gabriel continued on. "There are endless illusions. Even when you know the truth, it is hard to remember that the most difficult part of doing good things and making right choices is the choice itself. In making right decisions, especially early in your assignment, you will be impacted by the concept. One that is nicely packaged by the dark side is that you are alone and must do right, unaided. It will be difficult to understand that after the choice, you will be empowered by the Omniscient One for you have chosen Him. Life tricks you. For example, often it is more difficult and dangerous to descend from a difficult climb or hike than to ascend.

"If you go out on assignment," Gabriel cautioned, "you may succeed . . . only to find it is more difficult to survive a great achievement emotionally than it was to make the achievement. Human-to-human adulation is intoxicating, addicting, and can be ultimately corrupting. This is not a trivial point. Many have prospered and found their assignment and completed it successfully only to be foiled by the temptations that followed their success. That great philosopher-teacher Carpathian, on the planet Glancas, taught all the right principles and had a great following. His teaching brought peace and prosperity not only to his land but also to his entire planet. After he received great fame and fortune for his inspired contributions, he was elected to high office. He chose to deny the source of his inspiration and declared himself divine. Although the connection to the Creator was always available, Carpathian's choice to reject the Creator and his purpose cut off his source of inspiration and power. His last bit of life, and finally his death, was awful and not at all consistent with his teachings. His pain and suffering were brought on simply by his pride in himself. He became small, and in the end he was nothing. His success was his undoing. He did not come home to the continuum. To realize your contribution through inspiration is good, but to develop a false sense of power and importance, can be fatal. Do you understand this irony? It is not at all unusual for the Creator to send special emissaries whose mission it is to help and protect those who are on high-profile missions.

"Now I tell you a significant teaching in a renowned story of Firterra," Gabriel said with enthusiasm. "Consider that when Solomon, who was a great favorite in celestial space, went on assignment, he succeeded beyond expectations, but he was nearly seduced out of his achievements by craftily packaged trinkets.

"Oh beloved Solomon," Gabriel lamented. "How we adored him. He sincerely prayed to be gifted with wisdom. This request was the seed of the very gift he asked for. Here is a significant truth that you must understand. The seeking of truth, the pursuit of virtue, the request for wisdom, and studying to gain knowledge are the basis for and the only means to the ends."

Gabriel continued. "When Solomon became aware of his own uniqueness, he developed an arrogance that was not pretty. Many of his other projects after the temple were ingenious and beautiful but were frequently monuments to his ability more than to any other utility or higher purpose. Solomon got caught up in the intoxicating energy and intrigue of adulation. The addiction to the superficial nearly caused him to forget that the source of his wisdom, which was the basis for everything he was and had, did not exist in three simple dimensions. The farther he traveled from his source, the weaker he became, even as he appeared stronger, richer, and more powerful. He was nearly convinced of his own ability without the force of the Omnipotent One within him. He walked to the very precipice of his own demise, leaned over, and began his perilous descent.

"I tell you that there was gloom in celestial places as the light in his essence dimmed," intoned Gabriel. "A seemingly insignificant messenger was sent. Solomon was old and feeble when Deborah, an attractive young Hebrew chambermaid, was assigned to the royal quarters. After he attempted to seduce her, she rebuked him and reminded him of the source of his greatness. Deborah continued to encourage the old man to return to the source of the force that had made him great. She scorned his cynicism with her own simple wisdom, which was tempered with love, joy, and laughter. She gently turned aside each of his attempts to possess her. In time, Solomon's essence became slightly brighter. Finally, just before his second transformation, his essence shone brightly. Human history did not record the change and Deborah was forgotten."

Gabriel concluded his short parable of Solomon with this: "I can tell you that the cheers in my sector were as great when Deborah rejoined us as they were when Solomon returned. Deborah not only carried out her mission and passed her test, but she succeeded in assisting Solomon's return. Deborah's mission was to act and present Solomon with his options. She passed her test by delivering the message. Solomon's test required that he recognize, embrace, and proclaim the source of all his wealth, wisdom, and power. Deborah could have passed her test without succeeding. Solomon could not have!"

"There are other issues that you must be aware of," lectured the archangel Gabriel. "Wealth, power, and sex are not evil by themselves. It is when they become the goal and the end objective for accomplishment that they become evil. Plainly packaged accomplishments like loving and giving followed by honesty, defending the weak, resisting temptations, silence at times, and hard work, something you know nothing of here, are sometimes the foundations of greatness in both an individual and those around them. Not all assignments have the trappings of greatness. Some are strong supporting roles that are little understood. You must be prepared to handle such a mission and understand that it is no less of a great test. For example, a mother may provide the nurturing, teaching, and guiding that will both allow a child to discover their purpose and give that child the motivation to carry it out. Many times, even the individual in the supporting role does not recognize the significance or value of their action."

Again Gabriel roared, "Papoo, do not think that all assignments appear heroic! Some appear to be failures. Some tests conclude in what seem to be punishments . . . ignominious deaths by disease, starvation, hanging, assassination, and even crucifixion. You may be subjected to torture: emotional, intellectual, and even physical. These are things you know nothing of here in this perfection."

The great archangel continued the discussion with the ease of a seasoned parent talking to an adolescent offspring. "Sex . . . sex is something that you can only understand by comparing it to mind and soul melding together or separately. It is a unique third-dimension activity designed by the Creator to give third-dimensional, physical pleasure that makes the genders of humankind soul mates. They usually don't have much of an idea what it's all about beyond the three-dimensional physical pleasure. Nothing here can prepare you for the level of importance sex takes on in the place you desire to go. These beings are infatuated with it, and the majority of them do not really understand why.

"When you succeed in getting an assignment, go to Firterra. Begin your journey, and you will discover your assignment. You will likely have great difficulty in convincing many of them of your mission. You will likely encounter some societies that train each other not to believe in soul, essence, other dimensions, and the sense of their own timelessness. It is through various forms of religion that they try to address this problem. The many revelations sent by the Great One are in and out of acceptance and variously translated, interpreted, analyzed, and discussed. Simple acceptance of the provided knowledge is uncommon and often ridiculed. Even you may have trouble with discernment and understanding."

Gabriel continued in a firm tone. "Your success is not determined by the relative measures of the assignment environment but by the absolute standards of the Omniscient Creator. You must strive to succeed by the standards that will be presented to you as absolute. Accept no substitute measures. Alternative measures will temporarily motivate you to work for unsatisfying goals and will prove ultimately fatal if you persist in their pursuit. Do not get discouraged or disillusioned by false starts. They are the only paths to the assignment and are really learning events. Neither should you allow yourself to become troubled by discouraging and unsupportive comments about your journey and mission by those not in the slipstream. However, do be thoughtful about these comments. Ironically, do not be surprised if there are times when these negative inputs are used to give you guidance.

"You are conscious, in your present existence, of the Creator's omnipresence and His desire to be involved in your existence whenever you ask. The journey and the task you pursue will mask many of those things that are obvious to you now. The illusions of three-dimensional existence on Firterra are quite amusing from our vantage point because they are so transparent to us, but to millions of souls they are fatal both in their physical and spiritual dimensions."

Michael joined them and Gabriel continued the discussion. "It is most important that you spend some journey here and meander the continuum with Michael before you make your final acceptance of the assignment and embark upon the journey. He was very close to Lucifer before the fall. It is Michael who understands the mind of Lucifer in a strategic sense. When they were together, there were always games of discovery and attempts to read each other's mind when the communication bridges were closed. During the Great War, it was Michael who was chosen by the Creator to banish Lucifer and all the legions of the dark side from celestial space. He has monitored the Dark One continuously since then."

Michael had merely nodded assent until this point, but now he gave Papoo a long, penetrating look and said with gravity, in his strong melodious voice like was none other, "This is a very important mission. All of heaven desires your success. If you go to Firterra, it will be at a very critical point in their time."

The great field marshal of heaven elaborated. "Satan has changed his strategy to entrap human souls. The strategy of having a few evil leaders charge against what is good and who are characterized as evil has become transparent to the many whom he wishes to deceive. The old idea of a few nations—led by persons influenced by evil, dominating many souls, and fighting against nations representing the good that is in the human spirit—is not working like it used to. A new and fresh set of strategies is required. The packaging is magnificent and the logic alluring. It is not that the old is ever completely abandoned, but rather new strategies and tactics have to be added continuously to adapt to the evolving society and the individuals in it. It is Satan's strategy to upset the equilibrium of the planet, destroy it and all the creation on it. He is well on his way to success."

He continued. "You see, when the Creator finished his work there, he charged mankind with responsibility for the creation. The charge was meant to be one of trusteeship. It was not license to rape, pillage, and plunder the planet with complete disregard for the other creations. This particular creation is a special semiopen equilibrium system. Papoo, you have worked with several of these systems in your sector. You know that the several critical equilibria have great flexibility and are self-correcting unless relentlessly pushed to one side or the other of the equation. You will visit Firterra at a time when much of the planet is dominated by societies that do not choose to understand the importance of equilibrium. They are more than technically sophisticated enough to both understand and implement measures to affect the flow of life and the planet's equilibria. It is not their science or technology that is lacking; it is their spiritual retardation that does not permit them to see their connection with the Creator and the cosmos. Do not be discouraged. The time we are contemplating sending you to, and that you have volunteered for, is one in which there is an opportunity for an awakening to the incompleteness of existence without a significant spiritual dimension. There is great possibility for your mission's success. All the more reason for Satan to be vigilant and active."

"It is important for you to know," Michael added, "that Satan does not hate the creation. It is the Creator he hates, or really that he is jealous of, causing hate. The creation, loved by the Creator, is the instrument to be used to cause pain to the Creator. Indeed, the only way that the dark side can hurt the Great One is to deprive him of the company and love of that which He has created. When I fought Satan in the Great War, many times Satan expressed love to me and regret that I stood between him and his aspiration to be the Creator."

Papoo and Gabriel took their leave of the field marshal and traveled and were seen throughout the continuum. Gabriel pointed out many times to his friend the beauty of their existence and the cosmic value of their work. Papoo grew to love his work and the beings with whom he worked even more as he traveled the continuum. This travel and experience not only increased his affection for his current existence but also nurtured and strengthened his desire to take an assignment. One that was much riskier in order to help some of the Creator's other beautiful creations obtain their highest goals and the perfection of their essence so that he could return to the continuum after having served the Creator and exercised his free will. Gabriel related many examples of journeys that had both succeeded and failed. There were parables of those who were ultimate successes in spite of the failure of their mission and those who failed in spite of the success of their mission.

It was the latter, those who failed in spite of their mission's success, that concerned Papoo. Although he could not fathom, in his wildest imaginings, being separated from his essence, his very soul, by the illusions of a limited three-dimensional existence. He was beginning to acquire an appreciation for the enormity of the risk and the finality and infinite scope of the consequences. For the first time in his existence, he felt a tinge of fear. Fear was not a part of his angelic experience in the continuum. Nevertheless, he was drawn to the assignment in order to experience choice and experience the reward for success.

After much travel together and many discussions of successes and failures, Gabriel discussed the matter of Papoo's journey with the Creator. The Omniscient One concurred that it was time for the training to begin. Papoo would have four teachers: Gabriel, Michael, Raphael, and of course Melchizedek. Each would also do the relevant discussion of Satan and some analysis of his work as it related specifically to the journey and assignment. The training was to provide Papoo with all the information that he would need to discover his purpose and to tap into the help that he would need to succeed. The training would also thoroughly acquaint him with the risk of the assignment, such that he could opt out if he thought it too risky knowing that he might not retain the information. At the end of the instruction, Papoo would be given a final opportunity to choose the journey and the assignment or the eternal continuation and the current state of perfection in which he existed. If, at the end of his training, Papoo chose the journey and all that it included, the Creator would preside over the final lesson and Papoo's launch.

Orientation to Learning

Gabriel joined Papoo, who was in the middle of assisting a group of beings from Aerango. They had requested assistance in avoidance of a gravitational collision with a black hole, Trappus, into which they were being drawn. The great archangel smiled as he observed the strong, confident manner Papoo used in assisting the travelers and how he sent them calming energy to vanquish the fear that threatened to dominate their consciousness.

The archangel commented to Papoo, "You should be particularly cognizant of the willingness of some of these lovely beings to request help. In spite of what you may learn, the request for help is your most powerful tool in the quest that is pending for you. It is preceded in importance only by a willingness to be used on the mission."

At these words, Papoo instantly brightened and asked, "So you have spoken to the Creator on my behalf?"

"Yes, certainly," Gabriel replied. "He has approved your journey, set a course of learning, and designated instructors and a mark in the continuum for you to begin. If, after your instruction, you decide to accept the assignment."

"Of course I will accept. It is all that I have longed for throughout the continuum!" Papoo exclaimed excitedly as his energy level amped up and he glowed like a small star.

Gabriel concurred that the likelihood of his rejection of the assignment was remote. No one that he knew of had ever rejected an assignment after his or her training period.

"It is time to discuss the Creator's plan and begin immediate implementation," said Gabriel in a businesslike manner. "First, let me tell you that you are, indeed, getting an assignment on Firterra. You will be known to yourself and others in the three-dimensional time as *human*. You will journey to the latter part of what will be known to you there as the twentieth century. Time, in three dimensions, is a matter of measuring change. You will arrive about two thousand years after the Creator Himself visited this creation in order to help direct them, through direct teaching, to their perfection. As you now know, from the field marshal's information about this particular creation and the Great One's extreme love for them, the instruction that you receive will become much more detailed and tailored to the time and place of your assignment. It is a time of great expansion in scientific learning and technology. They are on the edge of many great advances that will, in fact, allow them to travel and experience the continuum, much as we do here. Yet there is considerable spiritual emptiness and frustration caused by the imbalance between spirituality and their material three-dimensional illusions. You may remember that these creatures were specifically created a little lower than the angels. Therefore we do have a great deal in common with them! Take note of this. I emphasize this because of its importance, and it is one of my most crucial instructional responsibilities. This state of being to which you go is designed to function in both the physical three dimensions and in the higher realm of spiritual essence. They all dwell in both states, many without understanding it. Upon successful conclusion of their journey, they will move on to the Eternal Continuum of Perfection. The understanding results from having the faith to believe in a few basic spiritual tenets taught by Jesus in His time among them and also by many others on journeys, such as the one that we are contemplating for you. It is not a change or understanding brought about by the individual creations. Rather, it is change brought about by the Creator. It is through the simple acts of faith and the growth to commitment and purpose that the Creator is allowed to infuse energy, peace, and understanding into their existence. Melchizedek will elaborate on this in his tutorial. Just remember you will not be different from those with whom you dwell. Having a divine purpose does not make you divine. All humans have divine purpose. Part of each individual's purpose is to help every other human succeed in his or her individual assignments. Enough of that." He sighed. "I am into the Chiz's stuff again."

"The Chiz?" replied Papoo. "I have not heard of him."

"Melchizedek," chuckled Gabriel. "He spends all of his continuum working with travelers. He doesn't socialize much. I can promise that you will learn to love him and his teachings. It is time to move on to an outline of your training program."

Gabriel proceeded with his explanation. "You will have four instructors throughout the continuum. Michael will instruct you in risk analysis, logic, critical thinking, paradox management, and finally strategies for success. All of these disciplines are necessary and critical to your success in the war that you will have to face and win against the illusions that will be created by the dark side. You must learn and imprint these lessons on your soul in order for your mission to succeed and for you to get back here safely."

"Raphael," he continued, "will instruct you in the arts and time. The arts and time exhibit the powerful creative abilities built into humans. You may remember hearing that the Creator also created these beings in His own image. This is a reference, as you know, to the spiritual aspects of their makeup. I believe this is truly part of this assignment's attraction for you. Again, as you know, upon your successful return to this celestial dimension the Creator will share with you the secrets of creation and the Eternal Continuum of Perfection. But I digress. Raphael will also teach you an appreciation for the creative aspects of other things: engineering and design, construction trades, cooking, sewing, and, one of my personal favorites, stone cutting.

"I will teach you the sciences and the integration of all the various fundamental specialties you are learning. Each by itself has little value. It is only when all the skills and learnings are integrated that a being has understanding and wisdom. No being, aside from the Omnipotent One, can be an expert in everything. It is important, in fact it is critical, that you understand the high degree of integration of knowledge and skills that it takes to create lasting beauty and obtain wisdom.

"In addition, Michael and I will collaborate on an in-depth study of our old friend, now the essence of evil, Lucifer himself, now known as Satan. That will follow a well-traveled tutorial by the Chiz.

"Melchizedek is known to a few of us as the Chiz," Gabriel said with a broad smile. "Although I would wait until he offers the familiar name before I called him that, if I were you. It's not that he would care; it is more to humor the rest of us that are not so well developed in the caring arts as he. His teachings are very wise and really quite simple. He has given much of his energy to studying this creation so that he could help them succeed. Learn his teachings well. They are by far the most important of all and, should all else fail, they will lead you inductively to many right decisions even if your openness to our input in that dimension is impaired. Melchizedek will be your teacher of philosophy."

"We will teach you everything we can in the hope that during the course of your existence there you will get in touch with your essence. Be willing to submit yourself to the Creator's design." Gabriel stared solemnly at Papoo as he continued. "Take responsibility for the assignment. Return and assume your place in the Eternal Continuum of Perfection."

"I want to start your instruction with this: Enjoy your assignment. We have said much about the dangers and the responsibility of the journey, but we would all be remiss if we did not point out that life, your three-dimensional existence, is meant to be enjoyed. It is the gift of God. The design of the system is such that you should be able to truly enjoy most of the journey while accomplishing the task for which you are chosen. Likewise, the most joy will be achieved by being in the cosmic slipstream en route to your goal. Good luck in your learning. I will join you later in the process. I see Michael moving this way. Let your training begin. If you need me to discuss, test, or question, just call. Michael," said the smiling Gabriel, "he is all yours."

Michael's Teachings

Gabriel moved away and Michael took his place at Papoo's side. Michael was beaming! There was nothing that He enjoyed more than training beings to successfully thwart the destructive plans of the dark side. It was far better to win the war for souls on a direct individual basis than in open warfare.

In the last war, Michael had lost 10 percent of his legions by defection to the dark side before the battle began. By the time it was over, nearly one-third of the celestial population, at that point in the continuum, was lost to the dark side. It still caused Michael pain to think of it all. The loss of his brother, Lucifer, and the loss of so many of his legions were equally painful memories. He could not understand how and why Lucifer had made his choice. He had wondered once what imperfection in Lucifer had caused this to happen. He had tarried on this thought about the same way that he had on Satan's offer of commanding his legions as well as great personal power and wealth. To Michael, this was no comparison to the eternal perfection in which he now existed. Even though he had been little tempted by Satan's offer, he knew that this was not because, at that point, he was immune to temptation but because the temptation was minimized by his thorough understanding of the alternatives and the results of each choice. Michael had an understanding that eternal perfection and the achievement of eternal light were not to be missed because of what could be measured.

Since the great battle, Field Marshal Michael had dedicated himself to teaching travelers in the continuum the secrets of the temptations, deceptions, delusions, and illusions that the ingenious Dark One had designed and spread throughout the cosmos. He knew by experience that it was far better to win the war one soul battle at a time rather than engaging in pitched warfare. Indeed, it gave him joy to know that he was causing Satan constant agitation. It was Michael's yearning that one of these travelers would be able to turn the tide permanently against the dark side before it was too late and the final transformation occurred.

Michael observed Papoo in calm silence. "So you are bound for Firterra," he said as a statement rather than a question. "It is a place of great beauty. It is a finely crafted environment with an equilibrium that is delicate but resilient. However, when the system is pushed it can become quite violent in its attempts to restore equilibrium. You should enjoy your assignment there. Do not let the beauty of your surroundings trick you into believing that they are God. Let us commence with the lessons. The first lesson is what has come to be known here as the Job Lesson."

The great field marshal began. "Papoo, you may have heard some of the story. Let me tell it to you so that you can learn the lesson embodied in the story. Job was on a journey and doing well. He was in the cosmic slipstream. He was very prosperous, in a three-dimensional way, and was enjoying life. He kept in touch with his essence and the Creator at all times and was not given to asking for help only when things seemed to be out of control and no solution was obvious to him. He was always in touch. A very unusual traveler! In fact, he was doing such a fine job that the Satan took particular offense and challenged the Creator. The dark angel reasoned and argued that Job was following through because of the rewards he received in the time and space of the three dimensions. Furthermore, Satan stated that Job would forsake the assignment if the God he depended on would allow the dark angels to manipulate him. God reluctantly agreed but set Job's physical body off limits to the destruction that would follow. In the reign of terror that followed, the dark forces ravaged all of the wretched man's property and destroyed his family. All that he retained in life were his body and his friends, but he remained on his course because he had his mission in perfect focus. This of course enraged the dark side. Satan returned shortly with another petition and challenge for the Creator.

"Satan reasoned that Job stayed true and on course because he knew, after the storm was over, his wealth and position would be restored. That, of course, was not true. Job's only assurance was his faith that if he kept his allegiance to the Creator's purpose for him that his mission would be a success. That was his ultimate goal. In any case, Satan continued to tell God that he must allow Job's body to be ravaged. He reminded the Creator how large a role the physical body plays in life in three dimensions. Experience has shown that even some of those who had successfully completed a mission wanted to cling to their bodies rather than be freed of the limitation because the transformation was a great unknown. The move to the Eternal Continuum of Perfection was and is a subject of much discussion and thought for beings in three dimensions. Within the limitations of their lives, there was no proof of the transformation. The belief in the transformation was entirely based on faith developed from some memory retained in their essence from communication in the slipstream. Later on, in human time, the Creator made a special transformation to give guidance and assurance of the ultimate human transformation.

"Satan believed that Job's certainty of the transformation was problematic at best. He therefore believed that his challenge to wreak havoc on Job's body to see if Job would, in the end, just curse God and die was a reasonable gamble.

"I too thought this was a risky proposition. I had seen some of the torments inflicted on bodies. Although I, of course, have not experienced such feelings, my observation is that, because of the system integration of body, mind, and spirit, this can be a very successful attack on the soul. The only true escape from the pain is to shift more energy to essence. This will have one of two consequences, or both: healing energy will be released to the body or the focus will move to the transformation. Many times these beings get totally deceived and focus their own energy on the body. They get isolated from the slipstream, where the energy needed for their travel, either to health or transformation, is available."

Michael continued with a grave demeanor. "Job had a consistent and excellent track record of being in the slipstream. However, given the level of torments that I knew the legions of darkness would assault him with, I thought his chances of surviving this test only a little higher than average. I related my concerns to the Creator. He noted them but granted Satan the right to this final assault, with only the limitation of leaving Job with his life.

"The war upon Job was accomplished in stages. He was subjected to generally declining health and continuous pain throughout his body and overall fatigue. This continued for quite some time, but Job was unmoved. He kept on his journey. Much of the time we were unable to get much energy to him because of the constant dark forces around him. For a while, his friends encouraged him. As Job stayed his course, the dark side was angry and mounted a final terrible assault. He was subjected to a disease of the skin. The skin is the largest subsystem or organ in the human body and has the functions of being a major contributor to individual appearance as well as being a major sensory device and major piece of the system that maintains the overall comfort of the body. This was a most ingenious and brutal method of attack. Job's skin became a patchwork of sores, bleeding, and oozing foul-smelling fluids. He was ugly and in pain.

"To make matters worse," Michael solemnly intoned, "his wife and dearest friend advised him to curse his Creator and die. But, of course, a merciful death was not an option in this particular situation. In any case, the advice came from one that had been tricked into believing that this disease came from the light side rather than the darkness. We were prohibited by the agreement from sending healing energy. No medications of that time rendered healing or reduced the pain. Job's friends provided great additional mental anguish by admonishing him to ponder what wrong he had done to get such a frightful judgment from God. In the end, Job's faith in the Creator allowed him to prevail over the darkness.

"When the trial was over, Job's health, family, and wealth were restored. Job pondered and analyzed all that had happened and was understandably frustrated with the Creator for allowing or causing this to happen to him, and he addressed his concerns to the Creator.

"The Creator responded by challenging Job and by reminding him of his mortality and his ultimate need to be connected to Himself, the Creator, for the energy of the assignment and for the transformation to Eternal Perfection. The question that stunned me was when the Great One asked Job where he had been at the dawn of the creation of Firterra. At that moment,. Job understood the limits of three dimensions. I never thought the answers provided were enough to satisfy the curious mind. In fact, I envy the fact that upon successful completion of your mission you will learn the secrets of the infinite and forever.

"I don't think Job was satisfied at that moment in time, but he did get the point that it was not his responsibility to understand at that mark in the continuum or in his mind, at that moment in time in the three dimensions. Job apologized for the challenge. In the end, the dark forces were resoundingly defeated by Job's commitment to his assignment. He was restored to health and prosperity and was transformed to the Eternal Continuum of Perfection. Presumably, his questions have all been answered, or perhaps it no longer matters and the perfection is all the answer needed. I do not know this piece of the story. If you think you need to know before you go on your journey, you will have to ask the Creator at your final lesson, just before launch."

"In summary," the angel said with finality and emphatic certainty, "the lesson of this rather long story is quite simply to keep focused on the objective and remember to draw your energy and strength from the light. Remember that evil and disease were invented and inflicted by the dark side. Job was right that he had done nothing to deserve the pain and suffering he experienced. What he could not know then was that it was allowed for a greater purpose, which was to illustrate that humans can survive the greatest of tests if they are focused on the source of their energy. It is often said on Firterra of those who are true to their assignments that when life is at its worst, they are at their best."

Michael and Papoo traveled throughout the continuum and discussed the various strategies of the dark side. Examples of deception, illusion, deceit, and strategic misrepresentation with intent to delude and dupe were discussed, and examples were presented. Papoo was a most serious and attentive student.

Near the end of the curriculum, as Michael observed a dimming of the aura of his friend, he admonished Papoo to remember that the assignment was life in another dimension. It was a wonderful gift that was to be enjoyed and was not, in spite of their recent discussions and the examples, a problem to be solved.

Michael closed his session with Papoo with an admonition. "Since you may forget all but an impression of my teachings in your first transformation of the journey, I leave you with this most important instruction: Remember to stay in touch with your essence, stay focused on the assignment, practice asking for help, even when you do not think you need it. We are all looking forward to helping you achieve your mission. I will see you at launch. I see Raphael coming in to take you to travel through his delightful course."

Raphael requested some travel with Michael, as there were some problems in his sector on which he needed consultation with the field marshal.

Papoo was left to his thoughts. He was concerned about the knowledge he had recently acquired. The new awareness of the risk did not in the least persuade him to forgo the journey. He would certainly try to imprint in his essence the basic instructions for success. He told himself, *I must remember these lessons and especially to call for help.*

Raphael's Teachings

Raphael returned to bring Papoo back from his musings. Raphael said, "Let us begin our tour. Your lesson with me will be spent traveling, discussing, and observing the results of the creative urge and talent that the Creator expressed in and even bequeathed to some of his creations. We shall observe and learn to appreciate, as you may not have before, the arts and creativity. I will not dwell on the science in each, as I believe my dear friend Gabriel will be teaching you science. Let us first go to the edge of the cosmos. I think we may find the Creator at work there."

They journeyed through the continuum to the very edge of celestial space. The place they were visiting was easy to find as the light was so brilliant and all the beings they encountered had an extremely dazzling glow about them. They paused to watch. There was a crowd of beings around the Creator as He peered into the nothingness. The crowd murmured in awe and appreciation as stars and solar systems appeared before them. Papoo was dazzled and amazed.

"Let us move on to a recent and developing work," said Raphael as they began to travel.

In a farther place, they observed another developing system. It was a beautiful and perfectly operating system.

After much travel and the observation of the Creator's spectacular work, Papoo commented, "I had no idea that the cosmos was so large. I have never been more than four sectors from my home base before."

Raphael glowed and said, "Now I want you to see a place similar to where you are going. The difference is only that this race of beings is more developed and seems to have a stronger inclination to the light. They work together to protect each other from the influences of the dark side and are generally committed to each other. And their assignments are integrated and complementary to each other. The Chiz—oh, excuse me, Melchizedek—will give you more information on that aspect of life."

After their observations of a planet of harmoniously living and functioning beings, Raphael said, "We are going to Firterra next.

We will be doing a bit of something a few of us are familiar with as *retromation,* which is sometimes called *parallelmation.* We will be allowing part of ourselves to be moved to a three-dimensional-like state. The difference will be that beings in three dimensions will not be able to observe us. We will be subjected to muted sensory inputs. You and I will be able to communicate at either of our levels. We are going back to the dawn of Firterra's creation. This always excites me!"

Papoo was excited with him as they retroed down. Raphael counseled that this was a version of what would be experienced in life. The two moved about Firterra in various time periods, noting the condition of the planet, the art, and society. They moved close to the time of Papoo's proposed assignment. Papoo observed to Raphael that the planet was anxious and frightfully close to losing its system equilibrium in several crucial sectors. They also noted new creativity and some lost creativity. Many of the individuals seemed to be at a loss in regard to their purposes and relationships to each other. Some were still focused on the cosmic purpose, and there seemed to be a desire to learn the Creator's design for the system integration of society. It appeared to be a time of great opportunity.

They traveled throughout the planet. Villages and cities were viewed. Art and architecture were observed. They watched skilled craftspeople working and artists painting, building, making music, dancing, writing, cooking, sweeping, listening, and sewing. It became obvious that each was investing something of himself or herself in the art. In addition, many of the art forms were an expression of the artist's soul, including the mother lovingly cooking for her family, the farmer in his field, the musician pouring forth beauty in sound, the welder attaching the skeletal pieces of a building, and the stone cutter fastidiously extracting a form that fit a building perfectly.

"You will find on your journey here that an artist's willingness to express their soul and become vulnerable has great impact on the expression no matter what the art form," Raphael explained. "There is both pain and joy in the expression, but ultimately joy if the best possible effort is put forth."

They discussed at length through many travels and illustrations the chemistry of painting and cooking, the mathematics of construction, the physics of music and dance, and the biology, physiology, and botany of farming, gardening, and life. Raphael suddenly interrupted himself in a dissertation regarding an intricate detail of the physiological design parameters of the human foot to say, "I know you have heard, but let me remind you, that although Gabriel's favorite art form here is stone cutting, the Creator's favorite is carpentry. We know that He practiced the art when He traveled here. He really has never told us why though. Perhaps He will explain that mystery to you after your successful second transformation." Raphael glowed.

Papoo returned the glow and asked several questions relative to what he had seen and heard and added a few conclusions of his own based on his own accurate observations. Raphael concluded that his enthusiastic student was ready for the science of Gabriel and offered to get together with Papoo, Gabriel, and the other instructors if there was a need to help all the subject matter fit seamlessly together as it did in life. Raphael also expressed his concern about the knowledge of the subject matter staying with Papoo through the first transformation and early part of the journey. Finally, he reminded Papoo to express himself honestly and completely on his journey and ask for help often. "We will be there for you," he assured him.

The pair returned to their omnidimensional state and Gabriel appeared with an enthusiastic greeting.

Gabriel's Teachings

Papoo was thrilled to see his friend and his joy was reciprocated. They immediately began the travel and lessons.

"In the world to which you go, one of the things science attempts to explain is God," began Gabriel. "However, as you well know, God explains science, or perhaps it is better said the Creator is science. Perhaps you can help on this front when you get there, as you have been well schooled in the sciences and mathematics throughout your career here. I will expand on that training very little. Rather, it is my purpose to acquaint you with the state of the sciences at the time you will be arriving on Firterra. Let us start with creation and evolution. This is a fundamental problem, as they say, in your time. Individuals of learning cannot deny the facts, yet many also believe in the Creator. It seems like an irreconcilable conflict of belief versus fact. Yet the solution is truly quite simple. The Creator created. Evolution followed as a part of the creation. *Automation* they might call it, on a cosmic scale," Gabriel added.

Papoo said, "In my past studies, I thought this was spelled out quite clearly in their guidebook."

"Yes," agreed the archangel. "However, the writing is metaphorical and includes regular intervals of input to the system by the Creator. It seems logical and obvious to me. The periods of development are even specified, although metaphorically. I don't know where they think the energy, matter, order, and beauty in that system and the universe came from if not from the Creator. I can only understand and forgive them because I know that I have never understood the omniscience and always and forever aspects of God. I was with Lucifer when he asked for an explanation of His origin and the Creator replied, 'I am that I am.' There was something about the manner and the tone of the reply that was enough for me. Yet it was not enough for Lucifer, and I can only imagine what a difficult concept that must be for a being in three dimensions. Consider the superior knowledge, intimacy with the Creator, and experience of Satan, and realize that even he could neither understand nor accept the explanation. It is very unsporting of Lucifer to use a concept he does not understand himself to torment those beautiful and wonderful creatures. You will soon be one of them. Let this put some perspective on the personality you will have arrayed against you.

"Science in the time to which you go is also very focused on the science of matter rather than the science of energy. They know, as you do, that very little of three-dimensional objects is actually matter. In fact, the interstitial space in matter is nearly as vast from the human perspective as the space between stars. If it were not for the energy in the matter, there would be lumps of boring, featureless matter lying about the universe. This is the genius of the Creator. It will be up to the philosophers to challenge the thinking of science. Those in science have learned an unnatural preoccupation with what can be seen and measured with the available technology. It is the philosophers and physicists who are more comfortable dealing with subjects as complex and sometimes apparently esoteric as energy and its forms. Real advances will begin when they focus on their true source."

"Furthermore," Gabriel continued, "each system has an innate predisposition to improve itself. In the terms of your three-dimensional time, it is automated or programmed to improve."

They discussed the complex mathematics of matter and energy. Time travel from a three-dimensional perspective was a subject in much of their voyaging throughout the continuum. Gabriel and Papoo went through retromation as Gabriel demonstrated the more complex concepts of matter and energy. Gabriel illustrated how a slight alteration in the energy of a system made it quite invisible to observation in three dimensions. Gabriel continued the lessons with an in-depth discussion and travel demonstrations of equilibrium. He demonstrated both micro equilibrium and solar system macro equilibrium. They especially focused on the planetary equilibrium of Firterra and the negative shifts caused by some human activity. Papoo asked many questions in this area. Since he was going to travel there, he wanted to be as knowledgeable as possible so that he might be able to bring about positive changes in the environment, if that was to be his assignment.

Papoo was again an avid student full of insightful questions that helped his instructor teach. Papoo loved learning. He felt each bit of knowledge made him closer to the Creator. This seemed to be true of all the population of celestial space. There were seminars held on an ongoing basis throughout the continuum. Each sector seemed to have different subject matter experts, and there were all different sorts of travelers from throughout the cosmos in attendance at each. Papoo felt highly honored to have four of the most notable citizens of celestial space as his personal tutors. He felt a twinge of concern and nostalgia at the thought of leaving this perfection and all of his friends to take on the assignment. Still, the reward was worth the risk. Yet for all this travel and learning, he knew through retro that he might retain little, if any, of this knowledge through the first transformation and the acclamation period. Although the instructions in that time and dimension seemed quite clear, he had become painfully aware, through close observation, that many of the human creatures didn't understand the instructions. To make matters worse, he was beginning to understand Gabriel's evaluation of the risk. *I, Papoo, will be one of them. I will be beautiful, strong, wise, ugly, fragile, and ignorant. What a bundle of paradoxes I will be. Limited yet infinite. I must focus on the assignment from the moment I arrived on the planet. Oh, to attain the Eternal Continuum of Perfection!*

Papoo completed the Gabriel curriculum, and with complete joy he looked forward to meeting the sagacious philosopher Melchizedek.

The sage arrived shortly and was greeted with warm affection by Gabriel. "It has been much travel since I last crossed your path in the continuum," declared Gabriel wistfully. "I have missed your company."

"Yes," replied Melchizedek, "I have been conducting staff training sessions throughout the continuum. The Creator's ongoing work requires me to enlarge my fellowship to keep up with all the opportunities we have. It seems we are all focusing extra energy on Firterra again?"

Gabriel replied that this was so and that Michael's Agape Plan was raising much excitement within the team implementing it. It was believed that the human creatures might now be ready to adopt the ways of the light based on the instructions previously supplied by the Creator during His journey there.

"So," the Chiz replied, "Papoo will journey to Firterra with an assignment related to the Agape Plan?" The celestial overseer outlined to the philosopher what Papoo's assignment would be, if he should accept it, and Melchizedek immediately understood his role. He asked several questions about Papoo and his academic credentials and characteristics. He found out that Papoo was committed to learning and that he was coming to a thorough understanding of the environment and the risk of his assignment. He was less excited about the great reward and more focused on the mission.

"I think he has a great chance of success. Consistent with past missions of this sort, he does not know what his assignment will be yet. He will receive it in his final lesson with the Great One. I believe that your teachings are particularly important to this student because the human characteristics required for this mission are those that contain the qualities that must be delicately nurtured, for they can be used by the dark side to great advantage. Your lessons are the most important to the success of the mission. Papoo must be able to believe and communicate your lessons from the instructions on Firterra. Your colleagues on this instructional team have done all we can to help prepare Papoo to have the image of your lessons imprinted deep into his essence so that the principles you teach will not be lost in the first transformation or in the orientation period," Gabriel stated with enthusiasm, gravity, and anticipation.

"Very well," said the master philosopher. "I look forward to this assignment myself."

The Wisdom of Melchizedek

Papoo and Melchizedek immediately departed for the planet Gnivol and in the retroform mingled in the Gnivol society and traveled around the planet. Papoo was surprised at the order and peace in the society. The planet itself was in pristine physical condition, although it was substantially older than Firterra. The arbitrator of Delta III commented on the conditions and made observations and asked several questions contrasting and comparing Gnivol and Firterra. Melchizedek commented on Papoo's observations and added some comments of his own. After a complete tour of the planet in that time, the Chiz, as Melchizedek kindly requested that Papoo call him, said it was time to move back into an early historical period of the planet and this human society. They arrived at the targeted time. Papoo was struck by the similarities to Firterra's condition, but Gnivol's macro equilibrium was incredibly close to the self-destruct mode. Yet there seemed to be an air of optimism and unity in the society that was not present in Firterra. They slid slightly farther back and Papoo immediately sensed gloom and fatalism in the society. Not only was the planet an almost totally dysfunctional mess, with many systems out of synchronous equilibria, but also the society and people in it were self-destructing at an accelerating rate. Papoo and Melchizedek spent considerable time traveling about the planet and observing the physical and social environment.

"This is both the worst and best part of my course," offered the Chiz as they moved back into their original time slot on Gnivol. "Let me give you some background on this example. It is critical to your understanding of my lesson. First, please understand that my teachings are simple. There are no hidden meanings or special conditions. If you and many of your fellow creatures on Firterra apply the principles I teach, the results will be the same as those you have observed on Gnivol. I do not apologize for the simplicity, since I merely represent the Creator as I pass on to you this wisdom. I fully understand that, based on the complexity of all creation and all the various rules and laws relating to the maintenance of a perfectly functioning cosmos, the simplicity of my teaching seems to be a humorous paradox. Furthermore, your training as an arbitrator has allowed you to understand the hierarchy of universal laws so that you could manage all the special situations that confronted you in the course of your job responsibilities. You clearly excelled at your job. Your training and experience might even prompt you to judge this lesson to be trivial. Again, as those before have emphasized this lesson, I assure you that although what I say may seem obvious to you, it is not trivial. Imprint this lesson deeply and indelibly into your essence so that no matter what happens in your life, no storm or trauma that you encounter or experience will remove it or make it invisible."

Melchizedek continued the history. "The change in Gnivol was brought about when one last effort was made to save the planet and the creatures on it. At that time, we knew the planet as Evolon. We had tried many offensives to keep the influence of the dark side and its legions out. Even as we succeeded in minimizing the input from the force of darkness, the society and planet continued on a death spiral. Many had forgotten the basic instructions or abandoned them in despair. Others were unacquainted with the fundamental success factors. As soon as we understood the problem, we petitioned the Creator to allow us to implement a new initiative that we have come to call the Agape Plan. It required risking several new missions, but we felt the risk was worth the reward of saving millions from the darkness. The Omniscient One agreed to one more initiative. He had visited the planet Himself sometime before and the basics were in place with a few individuals still working toward success by practicing His tenets. We quickly assembled a team of volunteers, like yourself, and the Creator added to the team. We implemented the Agape Plan, and you can see the results."

"The mission was simple and direct," the Chiz continued. "Teach the people to love themselves, the Creator, and each other, giving to each other naturally following unconditional love. Several of the missions were successful. The impact upon society showed quickly. Crime diminished and terrorism came to a halt. Prosperity increased. Improvement was not immediately felt in the environment of the planet. However, the destructive changes came to an almost immediate halt as the population recognized where and how they were damaging their own existence and that of their fellow beings and offspring. There continued to be some wild and vicious storms that were destructive and tested the commitment of the people to their new course. As you can see, given a few years of the influence of the light, the planet has returned to a dynamic equilibrium and the society continues to evolve toward perfection. Perfection is a long way off, and the dark side still shows its ugly face frequently, but overall the society and environment are moving in a positive direction that is more in tune with the Creator's design. We believe that the time has come to implement the Agape Plan on Firterra."

Melchizedek continued. "The principles of my lesson and those of the plan are pretty much the same. I give you this preface because I know that your experience here in celestial space will lead you to believe, as it has others, that this lesson is not necessary. The principles seem obvious. I agree that they are, here in our omnidimensional existence; however, there is a problem understanding and implementing these principles in the three-dimensional state. The principles are these: Love unconditionally and give of yourself unconditionally. These principles benefit both the giver and the receiver, but the benefits accrue to the originator regardless of response of the receiver. Furthermore, the giver, the originator of the caring, is responsible for the initiation of the cycle. There is both philosophy and science at work in the grand design of these principles. First the philosophy, in the words of the Omniscient One: 'Perfect love eliminates all fear.' In the three-dimensional state on Firterra, that is very important, as fear is a useful tool to the dark side. Fear is the foundation of dysfunctional behavior that is disruptive and destructive to both the individuals experiencing it and the society around them. You cannot give or receive too much love. The truly marvelous part of the human creation design is that neither can you run out of love, as long as you are tapped into the source through your essence. Part of the genius of the design that includes eternal essence is that just as here in celestial space, love is available in unlimited quantities."

"Now," he continued, "the physics. As you already know, love is one of the forms of energy. While it is never destroyed, it can be and usually is transforming. Some transformations take more energy, in the form of love, than others. As you know from your mathematics, the results are generally a matter of exponential improvement. It is actually an imperfect mathematical model due to the many other variables in the mix, but in the long run it generally fits. I think this illustrates the point. There must be humans who will be the channels and distributors for the Creator to send His energy. Giving naturally follows loving. Giving is part of our nature here, and it is simply a matter of total involvement with each other and all of the ongoing activities of the cosmos. It is not so on Firterra. Giving and loving are choices. You will find that giving can result from an intellectual understanding of needs and the solutions needed. That is a secondary form of giving that is good but not as transforming as giving, which results from unconditional love. This discourse does not mean that love does not stimulate intellectual activity and analysis leading to problem solving. Rather, it is meant to distinguish between two different types of giving. It is not unusual for giving to transform the giver through love given in return by the receiver. Hence, it is often said on Firterra that 'It is better to give than to receive.'"

"But I do not understand this part," Papoo interrupted. "How and why is it so difficult for them to do that which costs them nothing and is their natural state of being anyway? It seems that it is simple to understand that you can best receive by giving and be loved by loving. It is the natural state of things."

The Chiz smiled wistfully and replied, "Well now, your questions get right to the core of the principles. As you know, I am teaching you from the Creator's principles and my own observations of human behavior. I have only experienced three dimensions through retromation, and simulation is not the same as being in the state. It is now my responsibility to tell you that although the three-dimensional state appears to be a simpler state of existence than ours, it presents many complex problems because of the illusions of that physical existence and the spin put on much of the human beings' perception. These complexities and difficulties are the very reason the Creator loves this particular creation so much. It is most unique. I myself challenged the design in the very beginning as being very risky. It is unlike all other creations in its complexity and the number of design variables. No other creation has an infinite set of variables of continuous choice. They call it free moral agency. The Creator agreed that the risk was great but suggested that it was also an opportunity for the population of celestial space to work together to bring as many back as would be willing. Gabriel has the lead on this project, with Raphael, Michael, and me completing the leadership team. We are assisted by several legions of dedicated angels from all parts of the continuum and with every skill and specialization imaginable.

"Now some specifics. You will hear of me when you get to Firterra." The Chiz smiled solemnly. "I visited once and shared these principles as the recipe for success both on Firterra and on the ultimate journey. The part that is recorded has to do with giving of the tangible, which solves tangible problems. I related the principle and explained that giving to your fellow beings to help them on their journey is, in fact, giving to the Creator. It adds to the number that will complete the journey and their mission successfully. In a design that is complex beyond my ability to understand, missions are planned so that millions of missions are integrated and a successfully completed mission can result in millions being aided in their journey. What is recorded, the principle of tithing is an excellent principle, and you cannot go wrong with its application. It is, however, incomplete if not integrated with the lesson I have just given you. All of these principles are recorded in the same document. You would be wise to study and follow it. There are many subjects discussed that are useful guides to your success. They include diet, health, psychology, morality, justice, science (energy and light), and of course the most basic of all these: instructions on loving and giving.

I give you this caveat not because I really understand it, but rather because I know how the dark side works on Firterra. Do not get caught up in working to obtain matter in the form of material things in three dimensions. Rather, focus on spreading energy."

"Well, yes, of course," Papoo blurted out. "I do not need any of the things in three dimensions to get back here, nor could I bring them on my second transformation anyway."

"That is the point." Melchizedek sighed. "Imprint it well on your essence. You *must* remember it. I believe that your personality will be quite vulnerable to that particular deception, as much of humanity is. Remember that the accumulation of the goods of three dimensions is not a measure of your success on your journey. There is no wrong attached to the acquisition and/or the accumulation of wealth, as long as it is secondary to your other activities. All those things that are valued on Firterra were put there for your enjoyment. Enjoy them. Just remember that they are not part of your essence. Enjoy the journey. Cherish the gift, and come back to us. Call if you need help. Do you have any questions?"

Papoo confessed that he did indeed have a growing list of questions, but he would save them for his final course with the Creator.

Gabriel, Raphael, Michael, and Melchizedek met near the event horizon of creation and basked in brilliance, ambiance, and love exuded by the Creator. They conferred briefly about Papoo's progress and unanimously and enthusiastically decided to recommend his final course and transformation to the Creator. Papoo would be an integral and crucial part of the Agape Plan, phase 3 on Firterra. Their main concern about Papoo was one of his strengths: self-reliance. It could and undoubtedly would be used against him. He might not call for or be open to help, and they all knew that he could not successfully complete the journey alone. They ardently hoped that they had taught him well to stay in touch with his essence and ask and listen for guidance.

Finally, Gabriel thundered, "Let us begin the execution of the plan!"

CHAPTER 2

THE CHOICE: THE CHALLENGE

On Terazaria, far from the center of the cosmos, near the edge of the expanding universe, as it is referred to by humans, four celestial beings gathered to discuss the campaign about to be launched: phase 3 of the Agape Plan. Gabriel, Raphael, Melchizedek, and Michael gathered to meet with the Creator to discuss the project and one of its individual leaders. Both individually and collectively as a team, they had done their best to teach Papoo the principal success factors for the journey and assignment as well as the principles of life. The best and most experienced instructors that the cosmos had to offer had instructed Papoo in science, mathematics, the arts, and philosophy, which included the subtleties of giving and loving. In other words, Papoo had quite simply received the best instruction ever available in existence in any dimension. Yet these four great teachers were still very concerned for the student. The Creator would give the final instructions.

Experience had shown that in spite of all the instruction, love, and power available to complete the missions, many failed. Each was heartbreak for both the individual failure and for those touched negatively or not energized positively because of the failure. Millions of contingencies had to be created by the Omniscient One in order to eliminate the possibility of total breakdown in human society due the lack of enough energy in the form of love. They had observed times in human history where even the humans were aware that something was tragically wrong and an expeditious change was needed to avert chaos.

As it had always been, the instruction and tutelage of the Creator was crucial and was the most likely to be imprinted on the essence of the student, the traveler, Papoo. Papoo waited in great excitement and happy anticipation for the arrival of the Creator. His imagination was running wild considering all the possibilities of what subjects the Creator would instruct him in. He had high hopes that the Great One would perhaps share a little bit of the secret of creation with him before he left on his journey. Perhaps he would learn from the Creator the principle of avoiding the risk of failure on the journey. Yes, he thought it was most likely the Omniscient One who would tell him the final secret of obtaining a successful mission outcome that his four dear friends and gifted instructors had withheld from him. Oh, yes, he fully realized that they did not withhold this critical piece of final information to tease him. Rather, it was simply the order of things that the Omniscient One would reveal the ultimate secret of success for this mission. Or perhaps He was the only one who knew?

Further consideration left Papoo somewhat shaken. He had seen other very important missions go awry. There had been excellent personnel selection, the best of superb preliminary instructions and extensive training with the final instruction by the Creator. Yet he had observed many near misses, both plus and minus as well as numerous failures. He could only think of one thing that each of these missions had in common, but . . . he must be missing something. Surely his analysis was too simple. There must be something else. Was a request, a cry for help, the only delineation between success and failure? Were planning and ingenious innovation of little use without the inspiration from essence? Even further consideration caused him great optimism. His mission was to Firterra at a time of great possibility. The cusp of progress was mathematically a time for exponential growth, an opportunity for a graphic change in the learning curve called progress.

This was just too important of a mission. There had to be a secret of success. The Creator and the legions of celestial beings would not let him fail! He just knew it! He also knew that he was a crucial element in the phase 3 plan. Papoo had the striking realization that his most important task now was to absolutely imprint this important tenet, whatever it was, on his essence for all time. He must never lose touch with what was probably the only way back to the continuum and the entrance to Eternal Perfection. These were some of the thoughts racing at light speed through the consciousness of Papoo as he began to experience a wave of optimism, elation, and even a deep sense of awe.

This sense of awe snapped Papoo out his reverie, and he realized that it heralded the approach of the Great One. There was a distinct change in the environment. There was a brightness and freshness about everything. Now he was truly excited! This was the realization of a desire that began at Papoo's earliest memory of consciousness, to learn from the Creator, to have a mission, to go on assignment, and to return to the Eternal Continuum of Perfection.

The Creator approached, and even in the omnidimensional state the intensity of the energy and the beauty, at first, made it difficult to perceive the Great One. As He approached, Papoo had a moment of doubt. Why should he leave this perfection? The sense of light, rightness, energy, and well-being that was always present in this continuum was greatly intensified when one was anywhere near the Great One. All of these thoughts and feelings caused him to have a doubt about risking it all for a mission to Firterra. His uncertainty was short lived as he thought of the adventure and rewards of a life assignment. He understood that the risk was, in fact, very ominous.

Nevertheless, it was with joyous anticipation that he approached the Creator. The Great One glowed in the purest white and brighter than the sun as He greeted Papoo with joy and surrounded him with love. There was silent attention by all of those in attendance as the Creator began to communicate with Papoo. They moved away from the small crowd and the Creator said, "It is my task, pleasure, and responsibility to share a few simple teachings that will assure the success of your journey and give it richness and meaning. Finally, I will be giving you your assignment for your life journey. The success of your mission has great meaning to me. Firterra is one of my favorite and riskiest creations. Your success will contribute to the restoration of spiritual balance, which will enhance the environmental equilibria of the planet. Both will lead to the minimization of the influence of the dark side and ultimately contribute to the demise of the influence of evil."

With His power resonating through His melodious voice, the Creator continued. "You know that I created and dearly loved Lucifer. He is no longer the bearer of light and has become Satan. Since he left this Eternal Continuum of Perfection, he has brought me great sorrow by corrupting my most beloved creations. This is a strategy designed by that great creative genius, which I created with great love and energy, to bring me such pain that I will renegotiate his fate on his terms.

"You need to know that even for Satan and all of the dark side, there are terms of reconciliation. The conditions are quite simple: repent, ask forgiveness for all the damage done, return, help repair rifts, and become that loyal and beautiful being that he once was. Then the great gulf between us will close. I will accept him and all his legions back. The light of the universe would increase. There is room enough in the perfection for all. It was designed to accommodate all of my creations and expands as my creations expand. They, like you, were designed to exist in connection to me and my love and energy. It is the separation from Me and the Eternal Continuum of Perfection that makes existence so difficult for Lucifer and his legions.

"As you have seen, the conditions on Firterra are deplorable and are reaching a crisis point. The planet's many equilibria have been nearly pushed to the breaking point. The flow of love and energy, in proportion to the needs, is at an all-time low. Many have turned to the dark side in their search for meaning and love. In that state of being, I can only reach out to them with extraordinary measures of love and leading. Although it is my will that the course be changed, I cannot and will not change it through the force of my energy and will. I have much of myself invested in this creation, and I have already gone to extraordinary lengths to lead these creations in the direction of the light because I have left them in harm's way. They are subjected to the direct and most powerful influence of the dark side. It has been my intent and desire that these creatures be given the choice between the way of light and the way of darkness. It grieves me that so many have been deceived by the dark side. I have a mission and a purpose for each and every soul on the planet. It is not just you or those who have assignments like yours from this continuum who are special. Individuals on Firterra have a special essence, and each has their own assignment. Each assignment is entwined with many others with each having the intent of helping one or many on their journey toward perfection. It is and always has been my wish that each individual essence should join Me here in the continuum. I am saddened that any end up separated from the light and energy of this existence. However, the choice is a part of the gift of life. I cannot choose the course of the journey for any of them, nor you, but there is a celestial plan for each."

The Great One paused and then said, "You have sufficient background for the journey, and it is likely that you will retain this only in your subconscious mind, although if you stay actively and consciously connected to your essence, you will have a much broader base of information upon which to live and act during your journey.

"I am going to tell you several principles that will help you on your journey." The Creator smiled as he began. "The first principle is about wisdom and an awareness of the activity in which you are engaged. Do not be arrogant on your journey. If you have a special insight or wisdom, and you will have, share it as opportunities present themselves. You are likely to be instrumental in another's successful journey. At the same time, you must recognize that individuals that are special surround you and many have something to add that will make your journey more enjoyable and successful. Understand that not everyone will think you helpful, much less wise; some will think you stupid or be threatened by you. Journey on. Others will water and fertilize the seeds you plant, or perhaps you will be watering, fertilizing, and pruning the work of earlier travelers. It is the way of life in the three-dimensional continuum. Be prepared to judge some of your work and journey a waste of time for others. There will still be a lesson in it for you. Learn to teach yourself through your essence.

"The second principle is the dual nature of disappointments. Disappointments will result from the loss of relationships or possessions or failure to possess something, failure to achieve some goal or form some relationship. Rejoice in the knowledge that you are alive and experiencing the full range of life that is available to you. Examine the reason for the feeling and emotions. Assure yourself that the cause is worthy of the feeling. If it is worthy, honestly experience the full breadth and depth of the emotion. If there is a lesson to be learned from the loss or the failure, learn it! Then journey on! There is joy and journey awaiting you. You must experience some grief in order to understand joy and happiness. You could not truly give or receive unconditional love without being sorrowful at the loss of the giver or recipient of such a gift. Therefore, I again counsel you to be sure that the event is worthy of the emotion."

The Creator continued with the third principle. "When you arrive at Firterra, you will have a desire to seek out your mission, although the trip there will result in your loss of the memory of much of what we are attempting to teach you. Pursue the course of your inner direction. Listen to your inner voice. There will be a great deal of teaching that will diminish your sensitivity to that inner direction and make you question its validity. Test your conscience and intuition; prove its pertinence, legitimacy, and worth to your journey. Then journey on! Pursue your mission as your first purpose, and do not be deceived by the illusions of logical and more desirable options presented to you by the dark side. These *options* will not bring you happiness or the success you will be seeking. Furthermore, these other options will not bring you back to this Eternal Continuum of Perfection and Me. Journey on, secure in the knowledge that I love you and desire to have you return here to me."

The Creator then explained the fourth principal of learning on the journey. "Learn to read the road signs on the journey. Because you have a purpose, you will have a natural desire for your assignment and its successful completion. While it is unique and special, it is neither greater nor lesser than any other assignment. It is yours! It will most likely be a difficult journey of discovery for you. As you have been told by each of your teachers, it is your very strengths that will take you into black holes of dead-end searches that will leave you frustrated and disappointed. For example, your drive for knowledge, while beneficial, will most likely lead you for a time to look for three-dimensional purpose, joy, and fulfillment. It will not be found there. What you now know, you must discover then. Do not be discouraged. There will be value in even the most painful experience. Journey on. Not only is help available for the asking, but also there are many signs that will be provided along the way. Many things that may seem coincidental must be examined thoughtfully. There are not coincidences in my creations. That would be, as you now know in your omnidimensional state, a contradiction of my very nature and essence. The great travelers learn to read the signs. Often, you will find the subtlest signs to be the most significant. Pleasure will be gained from the both the challenge of the learning and the learning itself."

The Creator spoke firmly as He challenged Papoo to analyze all of his observations. "Learn to question the obvious. Many great teachings on Firterra are incomplete. The obvious components of principles are identified but the connections that make the integration of the components whole are not understood or taught. This makes those teachings incomplete and sometimes dangerously invalid. Understand now that questioning will often not only not be rewarded, but it will be punished. Question anyway. Examine ideas with your essence. Draw your own conclusions, and validate them. Teach yourself lessons. Understand what you do not understand. Revisit those topics not understood, but always journey on."

The Eternal One smiled with joy as He said, "Love and be loved. Learn to love. Learn to be loved. Avoid hate and anger. They are manifestations of fear. I have said many times that perfect love casts out fear. You will find that written in the guidebooks on Firterra. Fear is not a creation of mine! The concepts of love and energy are difficult to understand in the three dimensions' limited perspective. The power of love is even more difficult to understand there, but learn you must. For it is only through love—mine and yours—that you or any of the many travelers on Firterra can succeed. There is no limit to the power of love. There are no dimensions to limit love. Learn this, and journey on. Learn it early in the journey. It will make the trip both easier and much more enjoyable. Remember that I love you. There will be times when you will experience unhappiness. No matter how bad you think your journey is going, or how far you are from the path that is best for you, I always love you. Talk to me. I am always where you are.

"I could continue on much more." The Creator softly continued. "But you have all the essential teachings and much more for a successful journey. I know that you are still wondering what the secret of success is. You have already been taught the secret. However, I will state it simply again. Stay connected to your very essence, listen to your inner voice, and stay in touch with Me. I know that it seems obvious and simple to you now. It will not be so obvious to you in three dimensions. Treasure this secret, and carry it with you on the trip to Firterra. Imprint it on your essence so that, if you do not remember, it will strike a chord in your consciousness when you find it in the guidebooks in your search for yourself.

"Now we are approaching the place in the continuum for your journey to begin if you accept the assignment." The Creator's voice was resonant and firm. "Your assignment is, as you know, on Firterra. It will be your task to go and spread love and learning on the planet. You will be one of many with some variation of this task. Firterra is approaching a shift in her equilibrium. There must be a restoration of love for each other and the creation that I have given these creatures to occupy and enjoy. You will see more specific guidance and information throughout the journey, if you accept the assignment and stay in contact with Me. In return for accepting the mission, you will be given the gift of life. The reward for your success will be joy and fulfillment on Firterra and a return trip to this perfection. Upon your return, you will be transformed to the Eternal Continuum of Perfection and you will be given the answers to all the questions you care to ask."

The Creator paused and spoke gravely. "Papoo, natural law arbitrator of Universe Delta III, what is your answer? Do you accept this assignment, and will you strive with the gift of life I give to fulfill your mission and return to Me, your teachers, and your friends here in the continuum? Furthermore, do you understand that the penalty for failure is the loss of the reward?"

The last statement caused Papoo to shudder momentarily. The penalty was so awful that he paused at the mere contemplation of it, but he remembered the significance of the assignment and its value to the Creator. He answered in strong confident tones. "Yes, I, Papoo, natural law arbitrator for Universe Delta III, resign my current assignment and accept the assignment on Firterra and the gift of life. I do fully understand the reward for success and the penalty for failure." Then he added wistfully, "Thank You for choosing me, Creator. I will do my very best for You, and I look forward to returning to the Eternal Continuum of Perfection. I also look forward to spending time learning the answers to the many questions that I now have and those that I will, no doubt, accumulate on the journey."

Without further ado, the Creator joyously declared the celebration to begin, and they adjourned to the transformation area.

CHAPTER 3

NOVUM LUNA: TRANSFORMATION, THE TRIP

It was with some fear, anticipation, and great expectancy that Papoo entered into the transformation area where his luminosity ebbed and amped as his emotions cycled. It was a special place, very secluded, and only the assigned and invited friends could enter. Xoderap, his best friend, was there to offer congratulations, best wishes, and the assurance that he would be ready to help if called upon. Of course, Michael and Gabriel were there to see him off and two score additional friends. Many were in his creation group, and others were friends with whom he had worked. All expressed great affection and a willingness to help if he ever needed it and could remember to ask.

Michael and Gabriel joined Papoo for some last consultation before the moment of transformation. Each friend communicated love, concern, and encouragement.

Gabriel said, "My dear friend, we have enjoyed many happy events together. You have assisted some of these mortals that you will be like, and all of those in the light have rejoiced at your success. You have battled evil when necessary but never confronted it, as you will in this new existence. Remember that Satan, my now lost and vicious brother, will be lurking and watching with the intent of trapping you. The temptations for you will be subtle. These will seldom appear to be difficult choices that have any consequences or long-term implications. There will sometimes be complex games of testing. You will be deluged with disappointments that will make it seem that you are on the wrong path. You will figuratively fall into black holes filled with dragons. There, if you ask for help, you will find your greatest strength. I am telling you now that there will be no test or any temptation that you cannot handle, if you will expand your strength by simply calling upon the Creator for help."

Gabriel nearly roared as he continued his last training speech. "Again, I am telling you a great truth. Your strength will be greatly magnified to handle the need when you ask. I and other friends will always be available to help when the Creator dispatches us to you. There will be grueling pain, both emotional and physical, which you have witnessed but never experienced. There are magnitudes of light-speed difference between seeing pain and experiencing it. Always the forces of the dark side will be lurking about to note your weaknesses and try you there.

You can help influence the balance between good and evil, and unfortunately it can go either way. The dark side will not only attempt to exploit your weakness but also more diabolically use your strengths against you and for the dark side. For example, we know that you are not likely to seek advice or assistance except when absolutely necessary because of your self-reliance. The necessity of calling for help, for you, will likely be moments of desperation, at least in the beginning of the journey. In this dimension, that is the result of a combination of confidence in your knowledge and abilities, independence, and even some stubbornness. In the three-dimensional state, too much reliance on self can become arrogance and weakness. We cannot possibly tell you all of the tests that will confront you. If we could and did, you would probably not be able to remember. It is more important that you remember that the Prince of Darkness has no equal except the Omniscient One. It is only with the empowerment of the Creator that any of us are able to outdo Satan. The Dark Prince is the master illusionist. You cannot hope to defeat or even barely resist him on your own. We know him well, and he can be the most beautiful of tempters or temptresses. Do not let your love for a game be your undoing! Should he choose to come after you himself, you must ask for help, and the Creator will come to your aid."

At last the Creator appeared. He surrounded Papoo with love and admonished him to stay in touch with his essence at every stage of the journey. He advised Papoo that a strong effort to know himself at the very beginning of the journey would help him retain the sense that he would need throughout the journey. The grave demeanor of the Omniscient One made Papoo pause to reconsider his decision and excitement, but he was compelled to go on with the transformation and ultimate journey. Again the Creator said, "Just call us when you need us. I will always be there, but you must remember to ask. I love you."

Papoo knew from his teachers that in the beginning he would feel a conscious entrapment by three dimensions. After the initial scare, if he should recover some of his former consciousness, he would be able to expand to his essence. The terror accompanying the sense of powerlessness must not overwhelm him. The entrapment is an illusion of the three dimensions. The illusion of time, being finite and limiting, would be the most troublesome. This translates in three dimensions to total fear of the end of life and existence if there is not a thorough understanding of the transformation process.

The journey requires a commitment to remembrance of essence and a need to respect spirituality. Perfect love and spiritual growth will fend off fear of that ending—death—by giving one both a conscious and unconscious sense of the eternal nature of one's essence. Again, he remembered that he must retain his spirituality and sense of mission in spite of learning that argues it to be nonsensical imagination. Papoo continued to run all that he had heard and learned through his mind. One of his biggest concerns was the need to recover some memory of his past and his learnings immediately following the transformation and during the initial trip to his destination.

The points that Papoo would need to remember seemed few and simple. Yet Papoo was impressed by the urgency in the words and tone of his friends and their true concern for his well-being, success, and even his survival of this journey.

The transformation time was drawing near, and Papoo was acutely aware of the love, affection, and concern of all who had gathered to see him transformed. He entered the final transformation area and experienced a deep peace in his soul, which contrasted with anxiety in his consciousness about his successful completion of the journey and the tasks and challenges awaiting him. The moment came as a slight jolt in his essence. The chamber shook, altering the time-space continuum beyond recognition.

At first, Papoo lost consciousness, and his connections to and awareness of all other beings were gone.

Gradually, some consciousness returned and he experienced feelings of imprisonment. Senses cut off. The cosmos . . . the universe changed . . . There was no communication in or out of his being. It was a flat, isolated, and colorless suspension compared to the multidimensional continuum that had been his existence for eons. For the first *time* ever, he felt small. He was in a full panic trying to move, attempting to send signals for help and receive some feedback. Finally, he wondered if he had been caught in a black hole. He had witnessed beings in black holes on many occasions and remembered the terror of their perception of time-space distortion. Surely this was a black hole . . . And yet there were no intense inputs, no rapid shifts or rifts in the continuum. *This must be a time inversion,* he thought.

The terror was rising. It was scary because he could not put together a stream of memories. Had he made a choice for the dark side and had the darkness overtaken him? Then he realized that there was no sense of gloom or heaviness or darkness in his essence. His tension eased a bit with that conscious knowledge. Essence moved back to consciousness and away from the illusion. He reacted to the isolation he was now feeling. *I must escape from this trap, or I'll be doomed.* Doomed to or from what, he could not determine. And any plan for escape eluded him.

As some consciousness slowly returned to Papoo, he concluded that he was not the victim of a severe black hole entrapment. He began to sense rapid changes occurring in and around him. The terror subsided slightly as Papoo began to have a feeling of fluid warmth surrounding him. This feeling was intense and unlike anything ever sensed by him before. He felt a slight shudder as change occurred that he could neither understand nor control. With great and grim determination, Papoo controlled the fear that had almost overcome him. Slowly, he realized that he was beginning something. It was impossible to grasp the entire scope of the situation with such limited perception and with the tremendous intensity of change going on within and around him. This was definitely not a black-hole experience.

Papoo was thinking and remembering. Trying to remember. Trying to remember what? There was something before this. Papoo thought, *I was something before this. I have experiences that I can remember. What am I? Where have I been and what has happened that I cannot remember? Why are my senses cut off or just some of them? Am I trapped in a black hole? Where are you, Gabriel? Who is Gabriel? Who am I? I have a feeling of support and love at the mere thought of the name. But who in creation is Gabriel, and what is creation? I feel movement, but I cannot cause it. This is all so confusing. Great One, where are you when I need you? I'm trapped in some kind of simulated black-hole experience the likes of which I've never trained for. But wait, what is this? Great One, Creator? Now this is something, a mere fragment of memory. Gabriel and Creator, who are you? Come to me now. Show yourselves!*

A powerful change in the warm, fluid environment anticipated a change and an observing silent presence. Shortly, there followed a stern and terrifying, sinister, gothic heaviness of a menacing presence. The presence was a very different environmental influence. What was it?

Creatorrrrr! Papoo thought, and his senses cleared. *This is strange. I cannot tell who I am or where I am or what is happening, and yet I can detect changes in my surroundings and I can even influence them by thinking. Ohhh . . . aahhh . . . This is a rough ride. They could have given me a smoother ride. Now there is another of those thoughts. Who are they and what kind of a ride is this anyway? Creator, speak to me. I need to understand what is going on here. In fact, I need to understand all things because I don't even know who I am or from whence my thoughts arise. I certainly do not know where I got this knowledge of you, Creator, except that I know you are good and I don't know how I know or why I think that. Speak to me, if you are really there! No voice?* A bright, mystical, and hauntingly beautiful sense of elation enveloped Papoo. *Ahhhh, yes, that's more like it, Creator. Now explain to me what is going on here. Whoa, a sense of emptiness and sadness. Now this is strange. I need to analyze my thought fragments. So far I have Gabriel, Creator, they, ride, and some other uninvited sense or essence, whatever that is. It isn't much to work on, but I can't seem to do much on this ah, ohhh, bumpy ride . . . whatever that is. This is so confusing. I think things that I don't even know what I'm thinking or from what basis the thoughts come. From what experience do I think this? What is experience?*

Papoo's thoughts continued. *What can I sense? It is a warm and fluid-like environment in which I find myself. What is a fluid and what is a sensation? Where I get this description and interpretation from, I do not know. I have no image perception. My senses are severely limited. I cannot sense objects or beings, except there was that one change in sense when I called upon Creator when I detected evil. The darkness. How do I know this? So, it is likely that I have encountered, or at least sensed, two beings. One good and calming, the other fearsome and evil. How is it that I know these concepts of good and evil? So the question is: How or do I have a relationship with these two? Why are they here, on this trip, with me? So how do I know what a relationship is? I have questions. Creator, I seem to know that you are good and near. Help me understand. Come answer all my questions! Where do the thoughts come from? What is their basis? What is my experience? What is experience, and what is it I sense that I almost know? I'll just sleep a little now while I wait for your answers. Sleep, but what is sleep? Have I ever done this before? I do not even know from whence my thoughts and meager consciousness arise. This is totally beyond anything I have ever been trained for! Why can't I move out of this area of vacuum consciousness? Someone come and assist me!*

Oh Mighty One, come to me. I am on the edge of panic and have no understanding of what is going on. Help me understand. This is a desperate situation. Without your help, I may not survive. I may not survive anyway. Where am I? I have no sense of what is going on. I cannot even move.

A deep sense of well-being began to overcome his limited consciousness. A sense of meeting another being on this journey that had also been cut off from its native environment. Whatever was or is that? While there wasn't exactly a direct communication, Papoo sensed that he was in the presence of those who had a deep sense of empathy for him and were watching over him and waiting for him to develop. With a renewed sense of security and warmth, he fell asleep.

He awakened with heightened sensitivity of himself and a low-grade sense of foreboding. Clearly, existence was occurring in a way that he had never encountered before. Papoo pondered his conscious memory for clues to his current situation. Little was stored there that helped, or at least it was not directly accessible upon command. He was aware that he had a past existence. Memory was vague and uncertain, but there seemed to be patterns emerging. They suggested following instinct or intuition in communication matters that related to help and a feeling of well-being. This would not be the last time this communication thing and the logic were pondered.

In an effort to gather information and put together what was happening, Papoo made an emotional decision to expand himself by just letting his mind wander and see how his senses and the fragments of memories might come together.

He was later to learn that he had transitioned from a logical to an intuitive process. In addition, he was to have education in the scientific method of analysis. There was little respect for intuition among the scientists who considered themselves to be the true analyticals. However, by the time he had this learning, much of the intuitive had already been integrated into his being. He learned later to mistrust intuition, but after some scientific proofs of its value and validity he again trusted the strong sense of intuition with which he had been gifted.

Using this method of thought formation, his base of information began to expand at a faster rate. One of the first things that came to Papoo was an embryonic sense of purpose and the realization that he was on a journey. The purpose of the journey and the destination remained a mystery, although much thought was given to understanding both.

In a physical way, Papoo noted that he was growing but at a slower rate as time went on. One of the advantages of this growth was increasing mobility within the chamber. Although movement was limited, range of motion increased with physical growth. He delighted in the ability to move and took every opportunity to move about in his warm, semistatic, fluid environment. There were occasional bumps and unfamiliar noises on the journey. As the trip continued, a feeling of being loved and cared for occurred.

There were times when Papoo felt overwhelmed by darkness, foreboding, heaviness, and insecurity. In these times, he frequently cried out for Gabriel or the Omniscient One. As the journey advanced, so did the traveler's ability to cope with some of the darkness and emotional discomfort along the way. In periods of darkness and uncertainty, Papoo found that it helped to think of the light and the things that he knew were true.

Papoo sensed that he was not alone on this journey. Although he could not see the *others* in any way, he was aware of their presence. He was also aware that they were aware of him, and he knew that the others, or at least most of them, loved him, and he sensed their affection. Who exactly these others were continued to be a mystery. There were occasions when the communication and energy flow from these others was not exactly positive and supportive. This caused confusion to Papoo, as this information did not fit into a natural order in his mind. There did seem to be a relationship between negative input from the others and the gloom he had experienced as a sense of heaviness early in the trip. In addition, there seemed to be a diminishing of the lightness in the environment when the gloom and negative vibrations were in evidence.

As his knowledge base expanded, his body, as he came to refer to his physical being, also grew. Or was it as his body grew, his consciousness expanded? He was not quite sure, and this became a great question of his existence. Although throughout the journey he was to observe the growth of a body and a *mind*, as he came to refer to his thoughts he would never be sure which was leading and/ or controlling the development. He later decided that perhaps the greatest mystery was whether one caused the other or if there was some other, as yet undiscovered, cause for the development process. Surely the Omniscient One played some part, but on what level and in what detail?

Increased movement and expanding sensory inputs were a source of continuous delight to Papoo as the journey unfolded. However, there was an ever changing situation in the environment. His space sometimes seemed to change shape, but there did not always seem to be motion. Papoo had a vague memory of projection and of relocation without an actual sense of travel and motion. Some things on this journey just required more thought time to find answers and conclusions. Papoo decided that he would continue to work on these mysteries or interesting problems as he saw them, as time and/or new facts permitted or indicated.

As the journey continued, Papoo had the sense that either he was continuing to get larger or the compartment he was in was getting smaller. Quarters seemed to be getting more cramped, and as he pushed on one limit of his compartment, another collapsed on him. Freedom of movement became more restricted even as he seemed more capable of an ever widening range of motion. At some moments, and for some periods of time, the original primal fear returned because of his ignorance of his situation and environment. Usually, he found this fear to be unsubstantiated and it abated with mere thoughts of the Great One. However, sometimes this fear was strengthened, if not originated, by an outside energy that was negative and even fearsome. This fear and foreboding was not always the same. Although there were some common characteristics, Papoo was able to discern differences, as if a different but similar negative energy was generated by different beings. *Beings?* Papoo was sometimes uncertain he even knew what beings were. He had a sense that he had once been a being. So what did that make him now? If he could remember some beings but was not himself a being, where did that put him?

Is this a continuation of a past, or is this a new beginning with just a small amount of initial programming? Or is it a combination of both? But how could that be? His periods of hard thinking left him exhausted and frustrated. It did, however, expand the aggregate accumulation of what he believed to be facts and truths.

Perhaps the most significant but most challenging conscious—well, almost conscious—change was the *dreams*. In times of sleep, Papoo began to dream. He dreamed of a place and an existence where he had almost unlimited knowledge. Where he was always loved and felt secure, and best of all he knew who he was, where he was, and who he was with. He always awoke from the dreams with a bit of a shudder, as it was fearsome to go instantly back to the unknown. It seemed that he could retain the feeling and knowledge of the dream for only a few seconds, and then it was gone. At best, only fragments remained, and Papoo, although he was always disappointed at the return, decided to make an effort to retain any fragment possible from that side journey to add to his base of information. He spent time analyzing these dreams. He wondered if they were illusions, imaginations, or real side journeys within a main journey. And, did any of this really make any sense? In those moments that were influenced by the darkness, he mused that perhaps he had failed at something and was being punished with this nothingness. Then again in moments of brightness, he felt a sense of adventure and even purpose. He chose to dwell on the possibility of adventure and purpose. When he sensed the presence of the Creator, he asked the question of purpose. While he sensed no definitive answer, he did feel encouragement that there was a purpose to this journey and that he must ride on to discover the reason.

As time progressed, Papoo sensed an immediate love around him. This love seemed to surround him, but he could not perceive from whom it came. The physical environment became increasingly restrictive. The dreams became a place to retreat to from the unknown. It seemed that he could sleep and dream almost at will. The beauty of dreams was that he just floated away to another reality. In that other reality, he did know that there seemed to be few bounds or restrictions on existence, and he wondered if this was, in fact, reality for some part of him that he could not define. There were moments when Papoo questioned which sets of perceptions were real and if they both could be reality in different ways. He didn't think he had enough information to figure it out.

As the journey progressed and his quarters seemed to be increasingly cramped, his returns from the dream journeys were sometimes scary, as it seemed the darkness awaited his return and it took some time to suppress the fear and reach out to the light and return to the other journey or consciousness or whatever the other state was. In order to test reality, Papoo tried to stay in the dream state and found that he could not dream indefinitely. However, he found that he could stay awake and sleep and not dream nearly indefinitely. Although he did not know what this told him exactly, he was finding a way of sorting out things that he could manage or even control and those he could not. It struck Papoo as somewhat humorous that he had decided to stay in the dream reality if he could, but he could not. The next time he decided to dream, he could not. All he could do was think about learning of his purpose. He decided there was a message for him in this existence. So he imprinted the thought indelibly in his mind that he must discover his purpose. He almost laughed at himself for this conscious decision and didn't know why he laughed. Was it joy, irony, or just silliness? No matter, he journeyed on.

Accommodations became uncomfortably restrictive, and the thought patterns became repetitive and almost circular. In any case, circuitous. Sleep and dreams provided an energizing reprieve from the unknown and the fear caused by uncertainty. A relationship was under development with a nearby being. The Creator seemed attentive and always provided a sense of light when called upon. Darkness always lurked nearby but did not seem as forbidding as it once had because of the knowledge that the light vanquished the darkness. The journey continued on almost interminably until Papoo awakened from his dream by a tremor.

There was no time for the usual shuddering, for he was moving and shaking. The entire chamber and vessel were shaking and contracting and expanding. Papoo was in extreme discomfort. Both fear and expectation were at the very front of his consciousness. This motion and change seemed to continue endlessly. There were moments when Papoo thought that he and the vessel would be destroyed as the motion and contractions seemed to cycle and become more violent. Papoo tried to enter the dream state but could not.

After a wrenching, violent seizure, the vessel jerked and compressed Papoo to the point that he thought the journey had ended. Then suddenly and unceremoniously he was expelled from both the chamber and the vessel at the same instant. At that same instant, his ability to perceive his environment was dramatically altered.

Although his mobility was limited and his communication almost nil, he knew that he was surrounded by many gigantic beings, some of whom projected love and others that were ambivalent. In addition, there was the continued perception of light and the threatening darkness. Papoo was not afraid. This was the next leg of the journey. He was out of the vessel that had brought him here. He was at his destination. He must find out the purpose for this trip. Before all of that, he must figure out the communication and transportation mystery here. These he would do, given a little time. The mission had begun. Papoo was excited; somewhere in his consciousness, he heard the words *journey on*.

CHAPTER 4

LANDING AND DISCOVERY

Papoo arrived on the planet Firterra. He was born and christened Christopher Daniel Bird. Papoo was only a little concerned as he took stock of his situation. He could observe beings, people, around him. He was moved from place to place, but he could not move himself, his body, around. Well, he could move his body, but he didn't go anyplace. He just could not make the body work like he wanted it to, and he wasn't really sure how it should work. When he was frustrated and tried to communicate, he could only make awful screeching noises. People around him made noises to him and each other, and they were so large. Papoo could not understand this communication except for the tone of approval or disapproval. On the occasion of one of his frustrated outbursts, Papoo noted that there was a response of both approval and disapproval by two different beings. This confused him slightly, but he didn't dwell on it. Although he did retain the situation for further thought as more information was gathered on this place. The pattern of sleeping, dreaming, and entering another dimension continued as it had on the journey to Firterra.

It was these dreams that sustained Papoo because he had a growing concern about his ability to survive on Firterra, let alone figure out his mission and fulfill it. He could not communicate effectively, although all of the giants around him seemed to communicate with each other. He just didn't get it. The beings around him were more than ten times his size, and they moved him around at will. When he grew weary of observing and trying to communicate, he retreated to the dreams. It was there that he communicated with what seemed to be his past and there he felt encouraged to go on and keep up the journey. There was a peace and confidence he felt in the dream state that he had never felt in the conscious state. It was as if in the dreams he was being carried forward on his journey by an unseen hand, or perhaps it was merely fate. He returned from these dreams with renewed hope and determination to communicate. He did communicate something, but neither he nor those around him could discern the meaning of his noises. These were frustrating times. Sometimes, on the return from the dreams, he screamed in fear at the suddenness and shock of the fall from the tunnel.

As time went on, Papoo developed a special relationship with another being and he learned, although he could not express it yet, that she was Mother. She called him Christopher. He guessed that she didn't know that he was Papoo because he hadn't been able to tell her. No matter. He knew that there was love between them. It wasn't long before Papoo began to think of himself as Christopher because everyone called him that. He hadn't quite mastered the art of communicating, although his past screeching had become more pleasing noises that were still unintelligible gurgles and chatter.

Gradually, he mastered a few short bits of communication. Still, he was frustrated at his lack of progress toward his objective. Progress? He could not progress if he did not know what the objective was! He was tired of being moved around without his consent. He was poked, hugged, noised at, and generally had existence with absolutely no input or control on his part. Papoo worked hard at trying to communicate and control his body so that he could manage his own movement. He was not successful.

Papoo grew extremely frustrated with his development and progress in finding and understanding his purpose. In exasperation, he decided that he no longer wished to "journey on." He therefore decided to retreat into the tunnel of his dreams and not return. For some time, he had fitful and unfulfilling sleep that only left him more upset and impatient to be *out of here*. At last, while thinking calmly and wistfully of what might have been on this journey and the mission that he had missed, he begged for the Creator's help and slipped into the tunnel. While Papoo did not remember, until many years later, this particular journey into the tunnel; however, when he returned, he had a very different perspective on his journey.

As Papoo entered the tunnel, four individuals with whom he was comfortable met him. He sensed loved and peace but also something else in their emanations and a sternness. A voice boomed out of the light, "Papoo, why are you running from your assignment?"

Papoo responded with the fire of anger. "What assignment? I cannot even communicate with these beings, let alone ask them about my assignment or get any guidance for the task. I have absolutely no control of my movement. These beings in this place I have been sent do not much care about my purpose or me. A few of them love me and care about me, but most are indifferent and some are openly and genuinely hostile. Furthermore, I sense the threatening presence of the dark side that is intent on my failure."

A chuckle came from the light, and the voice that reminded Papoo of someone he had known named Gabriel said, "Is that all?"

At this, Papoo was really angry and retorted, "You really don't have a clue what I have been through out there, do you?"

The response was a quiet, "No." It was not the response he expected, and Papoo was stunned at it. The "No" was expressed in a tone that expressed more than a picture, and in the reality of that consciousness it meant, "No, but I know One who does know. No, yet there is a collective wisdom to help. There is One who has been there and understands, and He has sent us to help you. No, you may not return; you have just begun and you must journey on. You are needed on Firterra." There was a timeless pause. Papoo was puzzled by his sense of so much from one word. *I must be missing something very important,* he thought. In that moment, his soul silently cried out for answers. In that silent plea was a sense that the answers were hidden and too complex for him to understand. He was not even sure where to start the questioning. At that moment, a coldness came over Papoo's soul, and a sense of isolation and fear. A shadow seemed to pass over the tunnel, and its brightness faded. Instantly, one of the beings in the tunnel began to quietly and firmly remind Papoo that the beginning of all the questions and answers was the simple request for help.

Now Papoo was truly shaken! How had he forgotten this most simple but most important tenet of the journey? At this thought moment, he heard another voice say, "We will continue to remind you. The Creator will provide you with many reminders of the availability and method of receiving help. Journey on."

Shortly after that, Christopher awakened with a shudder and a cry. He found himself in a strange place, surrounded by beings dressed in white who were speaking quietly to each other. They became attentive to him as he opened his eyes, and he realized that his body did not feel right. There was joy in his mother's face, and she hugged and kissed him. In spite of being sick, Christopher was glad to be awake and made a happy, gurgling sound that caused all of those around to smile and communicate enthusiastically to each other and to him.

Christopher recovered from that childhood illness. Although his childhood was, for the most part, unremarkable, there were a few incidents and events, as in each person's life, that uniquely shaped his thinking and worldview both as a child and as an adult.

His mother and father divorced shortly after Chris's second birthday. He always knew that his mother loved him. They developed a closeness that was both spiritual and psychic. Or perhaps it was just mother's intuition? She always seemed to sense his moments of crisis (at least until in adolescent anger he cut her off). She continued to love him unconditionally.

He routinely entered the tunnel as Papoo in his dreams. He always returned and was refreshed by the experience, although he remembered little of any of these dreams. Papoo never again, during childhood or even adolescence, entered the tunnel with the intent of staying.

Chris learned to talk and communicate and did so with enthusiasm. He loved to talk to and listen to everyone, young and old, men and women, boys and girls. He especially liked stories. He was fascinated by instructions for doing anything in life, but most things interested him only once. There were a few stories and instructions that particularly intrigued him. He thought about those a lot. He repeated them over and over in his mind to extract meaning that he suspected was there, but he couldn't quite manage to perceive. He was especially drawn to things spiritual and not easily observed.

Chris entered the public school system at the age of four and learned to read shortly thereafter. Books were a wonderful complement to his dreams. In books, dreams, and imagination, he fished, walked, flew, and learned from his absent father. Reading was a wonderful and effortless flight of fantasy, and Chris went through books as though he had been born to read. He simply loved to read all kinds of reading material: books, newspapers, Sunday school literature, children's and adults' books, magazines, product labels, anything. It was a quest. Chris was searching for answers and the meaning of life, his life. He was sure he knew the questions. It was only after he passed adolescence that he understood that the questions were usually more work than the answers.

Christopher's mother worked hard at a factory where she tolerated the sexual harassment that most young divorced women in 1950s America either tolerated or made their lives unbearable by trying to fight. The hard work and the obnoxious, undisciplined, and disrespectful men were only tolerable because she had Christopher. She showered him with love and dreams for his life and hers. She sometimes wistfully referred to a future with a man and father, of unknown origin, that would bring additional happiness to their lives. It was additional because they both were somewhat happy and content with life and each other, although both knew that there was something missing in their individual lives. In spite of his mom's obvious love and sufficient material goods, food, clothes, reading materials, and toys. Chris had moments in his early years when he cried himself to sleep because he had no father. His imagination had in no way altered his concept of his reality, except to make the emptiness, from a hole named *Father,* more acute. He was not quite whole in spite of his reading, dreams, and imaginations, and he knew it.

Christopher learned early, and well, that crying was not acceptable behavior in front of other people and soon ceased to see this as an appropriate outlet for any emotion. Furthermore, he learned that open and honest expressions of emotions like anger, disappointment, hate, and unbridled rage were neither acceptable nor *normal*. Some of these lessons were tested many times, and he never did quite master totally muting his anger or unbridled rage. He did learn to express his emotions in the socially acceptable and bland articulation of the times. He had an extensive vocabulary, which for his own amusement he used to spice up the verbal porridge he was obliged to tolerate and return in order to remain on the normal side of the sanity line.

For Christopher, real emotional expression, except to his mother with whom he was safe, was not a strength. Furthermore, before he was a teenager, he learned to mistrust all emotion. Occasional anger was his only outlet, and it felt good while frustrating Christopher with its irony and irrationality. He found that love and hate were difficult to harbor without expression bubbling to the surface for all to see. He worked diligently and consciously to mask especially these. He found that love was a good antidote for hate, and he sought to nurture love without really feeling it. For some unknown reason, this seemed like the only emotion of value. The only thing that distinguished love from any other feeling was the joy that it often brought to others and that occasional funny tingling that accompanied the recognition, especially the expression of it in the giver. He struggled throughout much of his life to nurture it inside himself without letting anyone else know it was there. *After all, might it be weakness?*

Chris learned the relative societal definitions of normal and sanity well. He did not like to be embarrassed by his own outbursts of passion, frustration, and anger or his occasional angry reactions to other people, no matter what they did or said. In short, he learned to act normal, most of the time, at almost any cost. He learned to explain away or apologize for his irrationality. He was not about to tolerate anyone's, especially those hypocritical adults' examination of his irrationality. He could say he was fine, that he was happy, with the best of those lying adults. He could play their pretend game. He knew that some of his work (i.e., schoolwork, verbal expression, and answers to questions) was great when they said it was bad or wrong, and he knew when his work and answers were poor even when they said they were good. He did not often think he was smart, even when he was told that he was, and he never thought he was dumb or useless when he was told that he was. He was acutely aware when he screwed up something, whether it was schoolwork or other things that were measured or simply things that were said that caused other people to react. He analyzed his words, thoughts, and deeds for learnings to get where he needed to go. His mind was always active. Watching and waiting like a cat to pounce on truths and lies and learnings. He could not understand when other people said they liked something or someone when they clearly did not and everything they were proclaimed the contradiction. He did not understand the people around him accepting these lies.

Perhaps he was different from everyone else. He learned, painfully, that whenever he acknowledged and expressed his different thoughts and opinions, he was often chastised. From this, he learned that there were some people who could be trusted, a few, and they needed to be tested thoroughly and periodically reaffirmed.

Christopher believed, at a very early age, that there was some meaning and/or purpose to life. He was encouraged in this thought by his mother, some of his teachers, and at his church.

The God story was one of those intriguing stories that really stimulated Chris's mind. The Christmas story was one of purpose and commitment, and it made him feel good, but it did not explain much to him personally.

Even though he was an independent person, going to kindergarten and speaking his own mind, Christopher was awed at the enormity of the people and objects around him. Trees, buildings, and the first step onto the school bus were all huge. Streetlights seemed as distant as the stars. Mountains and the ocean were nearly incomprehensible, and since he had not seen them he imagined them to be fantastic and beyond anyone's mental grasp.

In the middle of Christopher's kindergarten year, his church was having special services for children. The services, of course, were focused on the teaching of Christian values and an experience with God that was the enabling energy to be true to those values. During one of these services, all of the children were invited to the altar to talk to God. Although he was younger than the age group invited, Chris felt compelled to joined the rest of the children in prayer and immediately felt a warm glowing presence around him. It was a marvelous and empowering free feeling. It seemed like a unique experience, perhaps even an epiphany. However, on later contemplation of the event, it seemed to him very much like his dreams as Papoo.

Although he did not think of this event as epiphany, or as an extremely unique experience for him, in later years Chris thought of it as the first conscious time that intersected with eternity and infinity. It was the first time outside the dreams that he consciously recognized his soul dimension and became one with it.

Christopher was not a very happy child or adolescent. It was with sadness and disappointment in himself that he journeyed on. He described himself as melancholy. It was not that he had no joy; rather, it was that there was no peace in his soul that life was as it should be and that he was focused on the objective. There was joy in achievement, such as reading a good book, a victory in sports, and a sunny day. *But there must be more,* he thought. He sensed that there was some purpose in life and he was missing the point. It seemed that his life was a journey without a destination. Sometimes, he thought that others knew the ultimate purpose and he did not. Occasionally, he questioned himself on how he could be so stupid about life while all around him people were happily living out their dreams. Which was? *Is it so simple I miss it? Am I too dumb to see it? Are others clueless and do not care? Do I not understand until I am older? What, what is the point of life? Surely it is too wonderful a gift to be an evolutionary achievement with only the survival of the fittest species as the outcome.* He pondered these questions of purpose and mortality endlessly.

Christopher developed his own philosophy regarding education, and it was quite different from that of the public schools. Basically, he decided that what he was being taught had little value for living and his reading had more real-life value. In the first few grades, he focused on the objectives presented to him and conformed to expectations for the right answers to questions both on tests and in conversation, and he was considered quite bright. By the fourth grade, the system was producing few useful answers for Christopher. He realized that the system was too big for him to actively resist. However, he decided that he would no longer conform. Christopher began to do the minimum amount of schoolwork and academic achievement to keep mom, dad (a stepdad had entered his life), and teachers off his back.

He pursued his own education. The school and public libraries were his life. He pursued learning by reading. For a few years, teachers continued to tell him that he was capable of better schoolwork and good grades and that he should *apply himself* better. He would smile or grimace and mumble that whoever was encouraging him was, of course, right, but he continued on his own course and became labeled a chronic academic underachiever, or whatever the politically correct description was at the time. These were quiet years for Christopher. No stellar athletic accomplishments. No brilliant academic achievements. There were no "My kid is an honor roll student" bumper stickers for his parents. He had only a few passionate emotional outbursts. Chris read voraciously and grew up on a farm watching plants and animals being planted, birthed, growing, and being harvested. He observed the cycle of life while wondering, dreaming, into the tunnel dreaming some more, going to church, wondering about God and an alleged purpose for each person, and revisiting the altar in search of the peace and purpose that he believed was available and could be found.

In vain, Christopher watched and waited for some friend or great teacher to answer all his questions. None appeared. There were times when he thought he might have found his mentor. Although each of these made a contribution to his growth, none proved to be a long-term guide. He did observe others following various persons whom they seemed to think had the answers. But Christopher saw too many inconsistencies and contradictions in their words and actions. He would have none of them. In addition, as Christopher observed the people in his church and their implementation of the philosophy they claimed to believe in, he was confused. The philosophy espoused and the actions Chris observed didn't seem very connected. However, there did seem to be value in the teaching, but he wasn't sure that it was very practical. Since church was a part of the family's life, Christopher continued the observation and even participation in the tradition.

Christopher did not think of church attendance as just a habit, rather it seemed good and right, but it really wasn't getting to any answers for him. In short, Christopher decided if "the way" was to be found, he must find it on his own. And he set about the pursuit.

At age twelve, Christopher realized that he was growing up poor. This, in his mind, was not a good thing. In his exploration of the world through books, he had already been exposed to the finest things the material world had to offer: great universities, art, architecture, music, homes, and palaces, not to mention the natural wonders and the beautiful people who were all a part of the world he had embraced through reading. It seemed that great achievements and wealth were the things that made happiness. Although the change in him had probably been subtle and ongoing for several years, this was a break-through time for Christopher. It was a benchmark time in a heretofore uneventful and unremarkable life.

The twelve-year-old Christopher Daniel Bird's own careful and pragmatic analysis of what he could do to take control of the course of his life produced some conclusions. He knew that he was not one of the beautiful people who could be successful because of good looks and charm. He was not a gifted athlete. He had no great talent. So what then did he have that he could build upon to escape this perceived poverty? The fact that he was even having these thoughts led him to the conclusion that he was reasonably smart, even though he now lived with the label of chronic academic underachiever. He smiled. He had even seen that phrase written down in reference to him. Furthermore, his underachievement had been explained to him as being the result of his parents' divorce and the emotional trauma it caused in him. A psychologist might have diagnosed this to be dysfunctional behavior that would be lifelong but could perhaps be treated with intense therapy. In fact, Christopher counseled himself. He told himself that he must shape up academically. He could and would become a scholar and exhibit intellectual excellence. It must be observed that at this point the achievement of superiority was now part of an increasingly more cynical mind-set. He had also decided that life was a game that most likely had an as yet undiscovered meaning and a purpose, both for collective and individual humanity.

Christopher made a solemn covenant with himself. *When I grow up, I will not be poor. If I ever have children, they will not want for the material things that I have lacked and longed for, and I will take them to the places that I have read about. They will know a better life than I have.* Finally, he promised, *I will find a way to make a difference, and I will make a contribution to humanity in this life. I will find the meaning of life and my purpose. I will win at the game.* This was a clear but simple and somewhat crude promise and an unsophisticated summary of a juvenile view of a present situation and future possibilities.

He started to encourage himself to develop superior learning habits and validate them by improving his grades. He sealed this covenant with himself by teaching himself to write backhand. His daily observation of his own unconventional handwriting would serve as a reminder of his commitment to himself to escape poverty and make his mark on Firterra—to accomplish his purpose!

Serendipitously, he was introduced to several learnings that helped him along this path. The first was about "positive thinking" from an adult book he found around the house and secretly read. The author's philosophy of believing in one's self and doing, rather than waiting for fate to help out, was groundbreaking work and made sense to Chris. At the time, Christopher had no real comprehension of the deep spiritual nature of this concept. His seventh-grade teacher pounded all of her underachievers with the value of the principle of self-discipline as a way of achieving, especially if one was not a gifted student. Since Christopher did not think of himself as a gifted student, this too made a lot of sense. Armed with enough self-confidence to believe that with enough self-discipline he could achieve academic excellence, indeed even superiority, Chris embarked upon a course that would become a significant segment of his journey.

His objective was simple and logical. He would excel academically and become an achiever. The result would be a prosperous career and job. He would not be poor. He detested poverty. He promised himself on his sacred backhand writing oath, that if he ever had his own children, they would not grow up poor. They would see and visit places as children that he could only read about now. He would tell them that their potential was limitless, and he would show them the way to success far greater than his own, whatever that meant and whatever that took. For now, he would study hard and plan the future as life offered up opportunities.

In the second semester of seventh grade, he began to make sacrifices and exhibit self-discipline in order to get the A grades that he craved. Chris was disciplined, and his reading was curtailed until all of his homework was done and he promised himself to cover all course material at least once before tests were given. He learned to cover the material as assigned, when assigned, because there were always sneaky teachers who thought it was cute to give pop quizzes just to show the importance of doing the work as they scheduled it. Chris learned to conform to others' expectations, and it was usually no problem as long as it got him what he wanted: A grades. His grades improved, and his achievement levels moved decisively toward the top of his class in some courses and above the middle in all of his classes. Christopher struggled often with the discipline necessary to do what his teachers expected and required for grades. He would rather have read what he wished and written the answers he thought were right and important rather those that others thought and taught. However, a few serious nicks at his pride and success curbed this independence enough for his successful improvement to continue.

There was pain along the way. There were times when he thought he had really good, even brilliant, ideas, which were sometimes contrary to or in addition to what he was taught. He passionately expressed himself. This behavior was not rewarded. In fact, it was often disciplined—sometimes subtly with a lower grade and sometimes with open ridicule. Christopher was not happy when he made an ass of himself and was embarrassed. Yet sometimes it seemed he couldn't help himself. When a teacher was wrong or was teaching balderdash, he felt compelled to challenge and assert his opinion. When chastised for this behavior, he was angry and vowed to himself to be silent. Yet often he was not successful in silencing himself. Christopher's growing stature as a student emboldened him intellectually and he began winning more arguments of the intellectual type; he began to more wisely choose the fields on which he would fight. On this matter, he learned some wisdom in the barn milking cows. His father said simply, "Don't get into a pissing contest with a skunk. You will never come out of that fight smelling like a rose." One of the applications of this was to not fight with teachers who had proven that they believed that they were omniscient. Chris just did not understand how people could be so set in their ways. He was always looking for truth and what was right and was constantly analyzing his own thoughts and philosophies. He adjusted them as new information came to light.

Chris's private thoughts on teachers were that the great (even just good) teachers were priceless jewels. Their passion for their students' learning and for their subjects had value beyond what they would ever be paid. However, bad teachers should simply be shot or at least expelled from the profession to eliminate the damage they were doing to fine young minds and spirits. He thought teachers were like horse trainers: some broke their charges while the really excellent ones motivated and sometimes even bonded with their malleable subjects.

He learned that there were sometimes penalties for one's past. For example, he was told by a counselor upon entering high school that he probably was not smart enough to do well in the college prep curriculum and he ought to sign up for general ed. Chris took this as a serious insult to what he thought he had achieved in the prior few months. He angrily challenged the counselor to let him try the tougher courses, and if he, Christopher Daniel Bird, failed, then the fault would be his and his alone. He did not fail. From this, he learned that counselors were not very smart and certainly could not be trusted with anything that was important to him. However, he did feel challenged to an even higher commitment to himself to achieve.

This part of the journey brought Christopher great joy. Excellent and competitive students surrounded him. Most of his teachers were skilled and committed to developing young minds. Most of his teachers embraced Christopher because of his obvious commitment to learning. Every subject now seemed interesting to Chris. Since he was a relative intellectual upstart, his peers were surprised to see his test scores at first sometimes, and then usually, above theirs. Christopher was thrilled! This was perhaps the reason for the journey? The learning itself was great reward but the A's and adulation for the achievement were real thrills, natural highs. He found new power in the ability to demand to be listened to, resulting from academic achievement, and this validation made perfect sense to him. Later, as he grew older, this would surely translate to other rewards and achievements. He was encouraged in this thought pattern by those around him, so he continued his journey on this course.

He was very intense about playing and winning the game of life, as he had defined it in his mind. Along the way, he learned the scientific method. State the hypothesis. Test the hypothesis. Reproduce the results precisely and accurately over and over. Exercise critical thinking. Ask what the exceptions are. Determine where there are the flaws in the logic. Do not, under any circumstances, get emotionally involved the experiment or observation! Intuition, what is that? Ah yes, that would be a relatively new study of something called ESP. This worked well for Chris. The scientific method was the perfect format to frame the quest of the inquiring mind. In addition, it was the perfect cover for the cynical mind. It, the scientific method, was a good reason to be skeptical about so many things. It was a perfectly crafted instrument to skewer all observable inconsistencies in other people's words, thoughts, and deeds.

Although he discussed it with very few people, the same methods and analyses that Christopher applied to others he applied even more mercilessly to himself. His lack of perfection bothered him. He constantly tinkered with his behaviors and personality to improve them to some standard of perfection that he imagined would make him the superior person he expected himself to be. Superior was to him a description of the best in whatever was being evaluated. Furthermore, he learned that everything in life was evaluated and measured by one's surroundings. Life was, in many ways, a popularity contest. He had the sense that this popularity thing was not always due to people liking or even respecting others. It was some phenomena that really defied his deep and thoughtful mental analysis. He spent time reading pop psychology and political analysis and just could not understand the popularity thing. He knew that he did not have it.

In a way, this popularity thing really did not matter much to Chris. By his own admission, he really didn't like people much. Most were ignorant, selfish, and self-absorbed. There was little that they could contribute to him and his journey, and he had no time for them. Of course, he did not, at this time, challenge his thinking or attitude on this. It never occurred to him that they might also be on a journey or that he might contribute to their success or that there might be any joy in all that relationship stuff. That was not logical. It just did not compute for him. It was not even considered more than a nanosecond. Hence, he developed few close friends. His friends were those who were well read and would venture to brainstorm important subjects, such as: Could there be or have been a God/Creator? Were there other dimensions of existence? Perhaps the soul was in the fourth dimension? Could one communicate with one's soul? If there was a God, could one communicate with Him, or perhaps it, and what was the meaning of life?

Christopher did not really even think about really liking his friends in any way beyond their ability to challenge his mind. He pragmatically believed that getting to the objective, the meaning of life, was what life was about. Certainly all that church bullshit was just that. As modern thought emerged and science advanced, the church would die as an institution. The church provided no avenue to or explanation for reaching God. It provided a comfortable dogma and tradition so long as one agreed with the dogma. You would have thought that there had been serious scientific study and the dogma had been proven, when really some old guys back in Hebrew and Roman times just wrote down a bunch of stuff that they had thought and talked about. These writers were all sort of connected through their ethnic culture or they socialized with each other. In fact, four of them wrote different accounts of the same story. Now credit must be given to their work as classic because of its endurance, and they merit study due those facts, good stuff, like Shakespeare. Still, Christopher did regularly attend church with his family. He dearly loved his family and he had decided to make an exception in not telling them what he really thought of this church crap. Yet there were times at church when it seemed that he entered another dimension and was at peace while at other times thoughts of soul and eternal essence and of good and evil were very unsettling. This was not logical, so he dismissed these occurrences as feelings and weakness of no value.

Oddly enough, it was Christopher's chemistry teacher who introduced his class to the serious study and consideration of paranormal phenomenon: visitors from outer space, ESP, dimensions beyond the third, and prophetic dreams, both uninduced and drug induced, such as southwest Indian shaman and doctor, Timothy Leary. Christopher remembered his dreams and one night, at the age of sixteen, he entered into the long-forgotten dream world as a sort of out-of-body experience where he witnessed the rest of his family watching television by passing through the walls of the house. When he awakened, he quickly went into the next room to observe them just as he had seen them in the dream. He questioned them and verified the program that they had been watching. He also, to the accompaniment of raised eyebrows and at the risk of appearing crazy, established that he had not been in the living room at the time of his dream. This struck Christopher as strange, metaphysics and science. It was not logical; yet the dream seemed natural enough to him. He could remember many dreams that were actually more remarkable, journeys out into the solar system and even discussion, communication, with other beings.

For some reason, Christopher felt that he had encountered a serious anomaly in his life and he had to discuss it with someone, but whom? Maybe this was some secret technique to the game of life? His revered chemistry teacher had introduced the subject of paranormal occurrences as a subject for serious thought. Perhaps he could be trusted. Over several weeks, Christopher sought out his teacher and discussed the paranormal with him at length. Were these things really possible and worthy of serious consideration, or were they just fashionable intellectual discussion of faddish topics? In fact, Chris learned consciously what he had read and already knew. These were, in fact, timeless and classic questions. But did the teacher really believe in the possibility of out-of-body, other-dimensional experience? Could he be trusted, and didn't everybody have these experiences? These questions troubled Christopher for several weeks until he discovered some answers.

Yes, the teacher really believed in the possibility of out-of-body, other-dimensional experiences. Yes, he could be trusted. Finally, after exposing his *secret*, Chris found that no, not everybody had these dreams. To be scared, elated, or just nothing was the question.

"So, what good are the dreams, and why do I have them?" he asked the teacher.

"I do not know," the teacher said, "but it is a gift, and you need to figure it out. Furthermore, I really think that there is a spiritual aspect to this."

This was the beginning of the serious mind games that Christopher would play and seek friendly but serious opposition for all his life.

A spiritual aspect? a thoughtful Christopher asked himself. He would have liked to dismiss the idea. But since he realized that he had had the same thought many times before, although not recently, and the person presenting the premise was credible, it must be considered and analyzed. Furthermore, what of that time when he was a little kid? That experience at church? He had never been quite sure whether it was a dream or a spiritual event. Were the dreams spiritual? Were those experiences dreams, or were they something else? And if so, what? While a lot of time and energy were spent thinking and reading on these things, no apparent answers emerged.

As Christopher continued trying to understand his dreams, he found that the Christian community certainly did not think the dreams were spiritual, unless of course they were prophetic! In fact, some Christians believed that they might even be witchcraft and/ or satanic. The scientific community did not think the paranormal to be spiritual. After all, where was the proof? These things were so hard to measure and reproduce, and history was full of documented charlatans along with the unexplained. Presumably, the unexplained was explainable; science simply had not discovered the explanation.

Despite his thought and research, Christopher was baffled. Was there a spiritual dimension, a soul, and an eternal essence? If so, wouldn't it make sense that this other dimension was accessible in life as well as in death? If this then was true, why wouldn't the spiritual community acknowledge and embrace it? It, one's essence, would seem to be always a part of a whole person and would truly make life a part of the eternal continuum. It seemed as if the religious community was heavy into dogma and tradition but not much spirituality. While some of the dogmas and traditions were culturally rich and some of it was even impressive, Christopher could observe little that related to the real issues of life really being accomplished in churches. There were the same human behaviors apparent in the church environment as were obvious in the rest of humanity because these people were not special or unique as they said that they were. Christopher's conclusion was a simple one: these people were hypocrites. In short, there were good, bad, and ugly in the church. Christopher's conclusion came somewhat later and was painful psychologically because it really was contrary to the teachings of his childhood and youth. The church and Christianity were time-honored traditions, to be respected as classics; any real value beyond that was uncertain at best.

It was true that Christianity and nearly all world religions, especially Native American cultures, espoused life after death. Yet there was no proof. While Christopher thought that in the long run the subject of spirituality deserved further study, there was no time. Science beckoned. Objective inquiry, investigation, verification, further questioning, and *proof*. Logic and order reigned. Science was probing the great questions of life and Christopher intended to be a part of the questioning and answering.

The path was logical and clear, and Christopher traveled down the questioning road of the disciplined critical thinker. The scientific method seemed to work well in all aspects of life, and in particular academics. He learned, or at least memorized, the prescribed items in classes and was rewarded with the expected A's that he highly valued. His writings for papers and essay questions were clear, logical, and articulate. These too were rewarded as expected. The bumps in the road at this time were the irrational feelings and anger that sometimes surfaced in his life. He often felt unbridled rage at inconsistencies and illogical behaviors in others and himself. It was especially bad when he was angry with himself. He dedicated himself to managing both the rages and the weakness in himself that were in the expression of feelings. Any teachings made available to him about feelings he dismissed as poppycock, unless they related to the control of his emotions.

Christopher nearly fell in love twice in high school. However, he had discovered what a powerful driver lust was. This he considered a weakness, because it gave another power over oneself and that was definitely bad, not to mention illogical. Christopher did pause to wonder, in moments of weakness, with powerful, agonizing, adolescent, lustful daydreams. *Are those teachings I have heard all my life about morality influencing me?* No matter. The danger of premature copulation could lead to parenthood, or even disease, and Christopher had things to learn and do and there was no time for such distraction. Each time that he was moved by infatuation, lust, or love, he would pause and savor the feeling. This often forced him to extract himself from the situation just before it was out of control. Sometimes, a romantic, dirty novel provided cathartic relief for his needs and was unquestionably justifiable in the search for truth and knowledge.

The four-year journey through high school came to an abrupt halt with graduation. It had been a journey filled with much success and joy of achievement and at least one bitter failure. Christopher had been nominated and elected to The Honor Society each of the four times since his junior year that he had been eligible. Each time, his high school principal vetoed his selection, which was his right as secondary school principals sponsored the society. It may not have helped Christopher's case that, when the principal had wanted to abandon the society as elitist, Christopher had led a grassroots fight by students to retain it. The principal's reasoning was that, in spite of the fact that Christopher was academically more than eligible and had been nominated and elected by his teachers, Christopher was not well rounded and did not seem to have an interest in anything but academics. Furthermore, he held no elected offices or performed any public service.

Since no explanation was offered to the young man, Christopher considered this lack of recognition a grave injustice and the principal an asshole. Had he been given the explanation, he would have agreed that he had little interest in extracurricular activities. Christopher would have agreed with the explanation, but he certainly would not have accepted it. Why would he be interested in any of those other things? He had done the analysis. He wasn't good at sports, music, drama, or public service. So why would he be interested? Public service indeed! He would have passionately challenged why anyone should need public service. It was clear to him that people should sit down and analyze themselves, determine what they were good at and what was possible, and then get on with it. He had done so at twelve years of age! No public service was needed! After all, wasn't the public library open and free to all? Wasn't public school required until age sixteen and free to all? What about self-reliance? He was self-reliant! He expected others to be self-reliant. He came from a self-reliant family. He was taught self-reliance at home, school, and church. He learned it well. He was also taught charity. Either he wasn't listening or he could not comprehend its relevance.

Although he received many other awards and accolades as a result of and in recognition of his achievements, he was angry and bitter about what he did not get. Unfortunately, he neither appreciated nor valued the honors he did receive. They were not part of his plan and did not matter.

Christopher took the college entrance exams and did well, just as he expected. His scores were in the top one to five percentiles. Christopher's high school grades and college entrance exam scores were so excellent that he was told by his high school counselor that he could probably go to any college or university that he chose. Since Christopher had already written him off as a complete idiot, he gave neither thought nor credibility to his counsel. In fact, it was not even considered counsel. It was nothing. It was not to be considered. Christopher Daniel Bird knew that he alone must and would analyze the situation and decide what must be done to get to the next level. It would surely be a struggle but he, Christopher Daniel Bird, was up to it. His applications to each of the several universities he applied to were accepted with congratulations and offers of aid, both financial and career counseling.

His parents, who had never been to college, guided him to a small church-related college. When the letter came from MIT offering to wave the application fee and offering financial aid and scholarships,

Christopher simply smiled and thought, *Wouldn't it be wonderful if I could really go there?* It simply did not enter into his thought process of possibilities that he could go there. He was self-reliant. He thought that he did not need to ask anyone; he knew his limitations. He really did not know his own potential or all of his possibilities. Although, of course, he thought he did. He would certainly not embarrass himself by setting up a scenario for failure. He had one bitter failure to his credit and did not seek to repeat the pain of that fiasco. He had no concept of a beginning that was not concluded with a success. Unfortunately, perhaps, his intelligence did not recognize his ignorance.

Just before graduation, Christopher had a most unsettling conversation with his favorite teacher and mentor. His favorite teacher called him in for an hour-long conference and Chris assumed that it would be graduation congratulations and good-luck soliloquy. Indeed it was, but it was not the speech that Chris had expected. The teacher started out with congratulations on his success and condolences on his disappointment at being left out of the society. He admonished Christopher not to dwell on this disappointment regardless of the fairness issue. Rather, Teacher offered encouragement to savor the successes. This was nice, very supportive. This teacher was truly a friend. At this point, however, the teacher turned serious, actually very grave. He said, "You have always been one of my best, brightest, and favorite students. I am embarrassed to say, however, that I have noticed something in you the last two years that really bothers me, and I must talk to you about it. Or I believe that I will have failed you."

Christopher was struck by fear. This then would be the discussion about his occasional rages (dysfunctional behavior?) and that he needed to deal with the cause, etc. etc. etc. Although they had discussed these things many times as interesting intellectual and scientific subjects, Teacher had never invaded this private and secret place that Christopher had hidden away. Christopher could not believe that this teacher would violate that space.

Christopher had grown to love Teacher as a true friend and mentor. He believed that Teacher was his guide to the next level. Young Christopher in fact naively hoped that perhaps Teacher would be able to explain the purpose of life. The many intellectual exercises that they had engaged in tested the limits of Christopher's thoughts and understanding. He hoped that one day, if he proved ready and worthy, Teacher might be the one to show him *the way*. For all that Christopher had learned from him, for who Teacher was and also who he might be, Christopher respected Teacher and loved him as completely as he was able to at that point in his journey. This discussion bewildered Christopher for much of the journey that followed.

Christopher sat in stunned silence as Teacher began. "You have been a wonderful student and a joy to teach. Your inquiring mind and your questions have been a joy to me. Our marvelous discussions of the paranormal and your descriptions of your own special experiences have been a true delight. What a pleasure it has been to have you in my classes and even, as you are about to graduate, to consider you a friend."

Oh, here it comes, thought Christopher. *Now that we are friends, he is going to use my bitterness and harangues about hypocrisy and the society to tell me to get rational about it and apply the scientific method that I have been taught to this situation and not be so emotional.*

As Christopher's quick and agile mind proceeded in front of Teacher on this course, Teacher said, "I fear that you have overlearned the scientific method."

Chris's mind came to a screeching halt and in staunch denial demanded clarification. He stuttered, "Wwwhhaaatt ddddid you say?"

Teacher looked squarely at him and said seriously again, "You have overlearned and misapplied the scientific method."

Christopher's heartbeat accelerated. His knees shook. His mind raced, and his eyes watered in a way that had not occurred in several years. His mind said, *There must be a mistake in his understanding of these words. It was too soon to draw a conclusion from them. These words must be tested and challenged. Indeed, this first translation must be a mistake!* He visualized a time, so long ago, when at the age of twelve he had pragmatically and efficiently analyzed his life and situation and determined what he must do. He was taught and discovered the scientific method. It had become his friend. It was his Magna Carta for life, discovery, and development. He blurted out, "What do you mean? You taught me! How could I overlearn? Surely you don't mean it the way it sounds!"

Teacher plowed forward. "You have abandoned all feeling and emotion for life as trivial and unimportant. You have great gifts of intuition and passion, among other things, and you treat them as if they were lepers or liars and were to be avoided and never trusted. There is more to life than logic and science! Don't you understand that life is a gift, not a problem to be solved? In spite of the advances in science, there are many questions to which there is no known answer. In fact, and I know this will make this conversation more painful to you, today's scientific facts are tomorrow's footnotes in history. You go to church. We have discussed what you have observed there many times, but I don't really know what you think about God and having a purpose in life. The scientific method will not, by itself, help you discover your purpose."

Christopher was in total shock and denial. He stumbled through his thoughts and managed to blurt out in disbelief, "This cannot be true!"

Teacher neither backed down nor wavered in the face of the angry intellectual onslaught of his favorite student. When Christopher had exhausted his entire considerable arsenal of logical arguments against using a more integrated philosophy for life, he smiled and said, "Teacher, I've got it. This is a test to see if I have really learned the scientific method. This is like a graduation test?"

Teacher grimaced and looked sadly downcast. He said, "Christopher, no, this is not a test or a mind game! I may have failed you. I cannot prove what I am telling you like a geometry theorem or a lab experiment, but if you observe life and seek spiritual truth, as I know you will, you will find facets of life that you have not accepted or experienced. You are very good at cognitive dissonance, the best I have ever seen. In spite of all you have read and seen thus far in your life, you accept only what is consistent and convenient for your own mind-set. If you are indeed a disciple of the scientific method, your inquiry will lead you to new conclusions and questions that will make your life more challenging and rewarding than you have ever imagined."

Teacher continued, his heart heavy with concern. "Finally, there are three things that I must ask of you. First, promise me that you will consider what I have told you with an open mind and work on it conscientiously. Second, learn to trust and use your intuition and the passion that often comes with it. Strong intuition is a wonderful gift, and you have a mega dose. Last but most important, do not reject love. Love has infinite value to both giver and receiver. I am troubled that the word and the concept do not seem to be part of the vocabulary of your life. Have a great journey, keep an open mind, and come back and see me sometime."

Christopher reluctantly and respectfully made a solemn promise to consider all that teacher had said and asked.

Christopher escaped from that meeting exhausted and confused. He lay awake that night trying to find ways to reject what was conveniently illogical, but from somewhere within him there was a sense that there was truth beyond pure science. He admitted to himself that none of his favorite literature was pure science. Literature was full of emotion and mystery. He smiled to himself as he considered that science alone made for a bland reading diet, and he did like a little spice in his reading diet!

So Chris embraced a new investigation and pondered his questions. This was a mystery to keep him occupied for the summer. He had much to consider before college started, much thinking to do, much reading to do, and decisions to be made. He believed that there must be a purpose to life beyond reproduction and the perpetuation of the species. But what, how to know, and didn't everybody wonder? If so, why wasn't there much talk of it, and where were the books to explain how to figure it out? He was frustrated, insecure, and excited all at the same time. *Surely, there must be a purpose in life and no doubt I will find it with the learned tutelage of great minds at college. After all, I am going to a religious, allegedly Christian, college, and there will be some of the great minds in both science and religion available to me. What could be better? I will start the journey now.* He thought this, and then began to read *War and Peace* for the third time.

Christopher's summer was spent reading, working, and contemplating that final lecture from his esteemed teacher. He attempted some definitions for himself in order to build hypotheses. For example, if one feels insecure, can one define what feeling secure is? Christopher was startled with his own answer. The time when his most secure feeling occurred was in his early childhood. It was a cold winter Sunday night in a warm church with the Life Saver peppermint smell of Mother's purse and the Life Saver that accompanied the odor. He remembered curling up on the pew and going to sleep after being covered with Mom's coat and being told that she loved him and that he was special. Chris smiled at the thought and wondered if the secret to that feeling was in the whole of the situation or one or more of its parts, or if the secret was in the dreams he sometimes experienced. He experimented. He bought peppermint Life Savers and found that their taste and smell evoked the memory, but unfortunately only a fleeting memory of the feeling. The rest of the experience . . . Well, it was not reasonably possible to replicate, except the sleeping in church, and he did that readily whenever he attended without producing any feeling. He did come to the very disturbing conclusion that the more he read, studied, was taught, and learned, the more confident he became, the more he felt and knew that there was more he did not know. This was another paradox he did not need to complicate his thinking!

What of one's purpose, the purpose of life? Is this feeling, my sense that I have a purpose, merely a delusion of grandeur? Is this spiritual or paranormal purpose idea just a delusional concept pursued by individuals in order add meaning to their otherwise empty lives?

The contradictions were so troublesome to Chris. Many educators taught that the inquiring mind and objective observation were the cornerstones of learning. Yet they became agitated and angry if their students questioned them. Some became punitive. A laughable paradox if it was not so detrimental to inquiring and creative minds. In the pursuit of justice, it seemed that objective observation and the scientific method were not always used to build theories for cases. Theories were often proposed and evidence sought to support conclusions rather than following evidence to the truth. There were many true stories of crimes being solved because someone followed the trail of intuition rather than the facts that were apparent. There were other stories of great miscarriages of justice when the apparent facts were used to construct illusions of the truth that sometimes obscured the truth for more than a lifetime. Another paradox. Then there was science. Yes, it seemed that many scientists formed conclusions and did research to support their pet theories rather than generating hypotheses and testing them or doing research and following the facts to the truth. Yet another paradox in what he thought should be solid foundation tenets for life.

In his mind Chris struggled to comprehend many questions, apparent contradictions, and paradoxes. *The truth? Indeed. Where is truth? Is there real truth? Can we know truth? If we do know the truth, will it really set us free? Science changes its facts as discoveries move the limits of our knowledge. The dogmas of religions change as society changes, or they lose followers and fade away. And politicians, their truth is really ageless . . . whatever got them elected and kept them in office. They seem to be only barometers for some social norms. What is real and what is true? Is teacher on to something? What is teacher's point? That even science is unscientific? What of that business about trusting and using intuition? That certainly isn't very scientific.*

Christopher's mind ruminated endlessly on the questions he had that far outnumbered answers. In his waking and in his sleeping, the questions rolled as if his mind had been caught up in a continuous loop. He dreamed the questions, and sometimes he dreamed of girls. He rarely entered the dream tunnel. *I don't understand or trust the dream tunnel.* It was too confusing. He went into the dream tunnel with questions, and they were answered . . . At least sometimes he felt they were answered; yet he could never remember the answers. He always seemed to feel different after those tunnel dreams.

Confusion became Christopher's intellectual and philosophical companion, and he scrambled to find some method of restoring order to his thoughts and his life. Purpose and truth were, if not illusions, at least illusory to him. Perhaps they were just whimsical concepts and all there was to life was the hedonism that he sometimes craved; yet mental indulgence and casual meddling in the sensual fruits provided nothing beyond a momentary diversion from the questions. It was not diversion that Christopher sought. It was answers to the secret of life and of his purpose in it that he sought. He was consumed with knowing the what, how, and why of everything.

Love? What of love? He knew Mother's love. He didn't have any particular conscious value for maternal love at that moment in time. For his part, he expected to give and receive love from his mother, and he did. His giving was out of respect and obligation, and he had no doubt that it was given back to him in the same way for the same reasons. His mother had become remote and stifling in the last few years. She did not understand him or his inquiring mind. Romantic love? This was a delicious treat that he had dwelt on many times. He decided that it was an illogical and senseless abyss that he was not about to fall into! Love for fellow man? How ridiculous! How could anyone with a brain in his or her head love or expect others to love their fellow man? What a bunch of idiots. *The majority of the human race really is pathetic. I am almost embarrassed to be a part of it.* Now again, he was aware of another of those irritating paradoxes. He was also oh so proud to be a human being with the right of self-determination and to be free. The trouble always came when he really thought on the concepts of freedom and self-determination. He would get frustrated because of the contradictions and paradoxes contained in them. For example, he had been told, after he had made the transformation from underachiever to brilliant student, that he had an obligation to use his gifts and talents to make the world a better place. That really annoyed him, and at the same time it perplexed him. He certainly had no talent, let alone gifts. His success was the result of determination and hard work, nothing more. So how could anyone get an obligation out of that? Besides, that was a contradiction of freedom. The concept of freedom included responsibility, another paradox. *It is just too confusing. This must be something I will learn in college.*

Christopher continued to analyze one more facet of love. *At least I can relate to loving myself,* he thought, but in the end there were no answers in thinking of self-love. He was a part of the human race. If the human race disgusted him, to be honest and consistent, he had to admit that he disgusted himself for the same reason that those around him disgusted him. He was imperfect. He was never able to accomplish everything he intended to in the way he intended. In spite of his self-discipline and usually calm demeanor, he was deeply infected with passions and emotions. No matter how he tried to steer the energy to logic and reality, he had feelings that were not logical and perceptions and dreams that were not provable or reproducible reality. He was in fact a hypocrite to the scientific method that he sincerely embraced and intended to be the mantra of his life. In that moment of conscious realization of who he was, in spite of what he intended to become, he nearly cried at his failure. Unfortunately, Christopher did not yet realize or appreciate the wonder of the integration and complexity of human life. Rather, he vowed to work ever harder to become the superior logical person that he had idealized. He would continue on and make the effort to evolve into his logical destiny. *But what might that be?* He would figure it out.

It was a lonely place to be in the continuum. Christopher made himself a virtual hermit spiritually and socially. He was wandering in his own desert. He searched, but there did not seem to be anyone to ask the questions that were so important to him. Teacher had his own questions and wasn't giving out many answers. Did teacher know the answers? Was he keeping them a secret? Chris did not think so. *If the issues confronting me are so urgent and in need of answers, why isn't everybody talking about it?* Christopher wondered in near panic. *Doesn't everybody want to know what the purpose and meaning of life is? Their life and their purpose?* Finally, there seemed no place to turn but inward unto himself.

Maybe, just maybe, I am crazy . . . Insane. Yes. Perhaps . . . Maybe I really am crazy. I have seriously screwed myself up. Why? Why, if knowing the purpose of life and consequently knowing one's own purpose is so important, don't people talk about it more?

His peers thought him weird to be so serious. Most of his elders told him to ask God for guidance or told him he would figure it out eventually. *Eventually* always seemed a long way off, and of course he had already asked God and concluded that God wasn't telling. Although there had been a few people who volunteered to speak as or for God, Christopher had no doubt that they were brainless idiots.

These were self-serving, fantasizing fanatics, and certainly they had no news for him from God.

His thoughts continued. *I'm only seventeen. I have graduated from high school with high honors. I am going to college, and I am going to be a doctor. Unfortunately, I do not know why about much of anything. These last four years have been fun. I have learned a lot. I have transformed myself into a respected person and student. I am well on the course that I have plotted. Therefore I will journey on.*

In his mind, he said, *I will consider the important paradoxes that I have learned, and I will consider Teacher's admonition because, as he said, I have a sense that he is on to something important. There is much to learn and many paradoxes out there.* One of Christopher's personal favorite paradoxes was that matter was composed of little substance but much interstitial space and energy . . . That integration concept again.

Reading didn't help. Christopher loved *War and Peace*, but it gave him no peace and he thought it should have been retitled *Life and Death*. He pursued lighter reading but continued the journey mentally. One night, in frustration, he cried out to a God he wasn't even sure he believed in (as he knew, lack of proof). He fell asleep and entered into the dream tunnel. When he awakened, for no good reason, he had an extremely optimistic outlook.

College

In four years of college, Christopher was not a party animal. In fact, he was the antithesis of the party animal. He was on a quest for answers. It occurred to him that it was logical that there might be a great mentor-teacher to show him the way, or at least the way to the answers. A guide would make the search so much easier. So he searched for both answers to his questions and a guide. It was a melancholy epoch for this traveler.

These were years of growth and change. Christopher exhibited his intellectual independence and paid somewhat dearly for it in lower grades. He learned what he already knew, that a good portion of academic grading was based on conformity to the rule of the expectation of syllabus: Follow the professor's outline, take notes, pretend each class is the most interesting and valuable material you have ever learned, and answer the professor's questions with the professor's answers. Christopher was not about to be bullied intellectually and was not, and he did not often conform. He was seldom rewarded for his independent thought. Nevertheless, he pursued learning with unrestrained passion. He also pursued a course that he started a foundation for at the age of twelve. In spite of his inquiring mind, it did not occur to him to revisit the fundamental plotting of the course for its appropriateness to his current position in the continuum of life or the journey.

He journeyed relentlessly on. He studied chemistry, mathematics, physics, and biology with a vengeance. He went to endless labs, solved problems, and produced concise lab reports. He worked interminable hours at jobs to support his learning habit. He studied into the wee hours of the morning, well past the time when he remembered why he was doing it all. Other courses proved to be interesting diversions: literature, history, German (to better read *Beilstien's Handbook of Organic Chemistry*), philosophy, and religion. Most proved to be interesting, but the religion classes were taught with doctrinal fervor, which Christopher thought appalling in the academic setting. He did become much more cognizant of the Scriptures and some of their meanings.

Because Christopher honored his pledge he had made to teacher upon leaving high school, he did try to keep his mind open to the possibility that multifaceted, integrated development might be appropriate in life. True to the scientific method, Christopher considered that the Bible might hold some keys to life, and he thought it should. Since he was now in college and much older and wiser than he had been a few years ago, Christopher seriously studied it as a possible guidebook for the pursuit and finding of his answers. After serious course and personal study, Christopher rejected it with disappointment and sadness. While the Good Book seemed to contain much of value, it also seemed full of contradictions, not to mention the heavy use of metaphor, simile, and allegory that made it difficult to understand. To further compound the problem, it was ancient writing by many authors, from many translations. Were the metaphors contradictions? The questions raised were many. He asked himself, *How exactly does one die to live? How is it that one gives to receive? No, either that is stupid or self-serving. You cannot possibly have it both ways.* Christopher judged biblical Christian teachings as impossible to understand, seldom practiced (if it were indeed possible or practical to live as was recommended), and even outdated. All that loving your fellow man rubbish didn't make sense when he had last thought about it in high school, and it had not improved with aging in any way that Christopher could logically recognize.

It was with a certain gothic heaviness and melancholy that Christopher abandoned Christianity and its teachings for any hope of answers beyond good basic ethics for all humanity. After all, if there was a God, where was he and why didn't he speak in that personal way that seemed to be promised in the Bible?

Although Christopher was philosophically disappointed in his progress on the journey, the objective of pursuing medical school remained to motivate him on to a goal. The objective remained, even after Christopher could no longer explain why it was the objective.

The beginning of a new segment in the journey began with a date with a girl who became a serious relationship. Love came into Christopher's life unexpectedly and unsought. It was an avalanche of emotion that he could neither understand nor free himself of. It was the most powerful force he had ever experienced, and he applied his intellect and energy to thwarting it or at least reducing its power over him. It was unplanned and most certainly weakness to be under its influence.

Being in love gave Christopher joy and happiness that he had never before experienced or dreamed of. In some ways, he had metamorphosed from introvert to extrovert. He thought constantly of his love and her needs. He spent every cent he had, unselfishly, on her. He despised himself for his weakness. He fought love. This was not right. It was the wrong time and the wrong person. She could never, as a musician . . . an artist, understand him, nor could he understand her. Furthermore, there was his list. Christopher did not think it inconsistent to judge love as weakness and useless while at the same time preparing for it. It was a matter of observing that it happened to nearly everybody, therefore it was best to be prepared. Hence, he had his list of desirable female attributes.

The list was quite comprehensive and was even often copied by Christopher's acquaintances. The list included valued physical attributes—body type, breast size, leg conformation—as well as a comprehensive documentation of the necessary skill sets for anyone aspiring to be his love.

The problems were many. Christopher was not looking for love. He didn't really believe in it. He was not pursuing happiness. He did not believe happiness was either achievable or real. He was seeking the answers to and the meaning of life. This young woman failed the test of the list. Still, he continued to love in complete contradiction to his intentions. During these days and weeks and months, Christopher would frequently awaken with a smile and tell himself that love was good today and that he would fall out of love tomorrow, as had always happened before. The months of being in love continued. Christopher, quite in spite of himself, fell in love again, this time with classical music, the specialty of this girl/woman. He was a total mess. His grades were in the toilet. His mind was either on the girl or on fighting love. His life was chaos.

Christopher was an emotional wreck and he had no idea how to cope with his dilemma. Nothing he had read, studied, or learned had prepared him for this moment and this situation. His life was perfect; his life was a wreck. Life was an ecstasy; life was hell. Those nasty paradoxes were in glaring evidence again. Christopher even vacillated into thoughts of embracing this love in his mind because it felt so good. Yet still it did not seem logical. Beyond his list, there was a bigger problem. What about *her* list? That no such thing existed did not occur to Christopher. While he did not want to be in love with her, he did not want her *not* to be in love with him. Was that really a contradiction too? In truth, how could he measure up to her list? No way! He could not measure up to her expectations. He had never really planned for this. How could she really love him? He could not see himself as lovable. He was bright and interesting, in short wonderful, maybe. Lovable? No. Was he potential husband and father material? No. He had not figured out his own childhood and how he felt about that. How could he possibly consider being a father to a child or, worse, children! These thoughts occupied all the mental space and energy he had. In addition, he had to live as if he were not an emotional cripple, which he knew that he was. He was overwhelmed by paradoxes, contradictions, and an emotional tsunami. Total confusion reigned.

Christopher barely managed to get accepted into medical school. His faltering senior grades and MCAT (Medical College Admission Test) scores were countered by strong recommendations from teachers, professors, and doctor acquaintances. Just before he signed a matriculation commitment to a fine medical school, he realized that he no longer cared about medicine. He was not sure why he had cared before, or why he now didn't care. Had the driving force simply been the challenge, the idea of a poor farm boy going to medical school? It was not love of fellow man. Christopher thought that his lack of love and compassion for his fellow man ought to disqualify him from being a doctor. Yet pragmatism might be a good thing; no emotions in very difficult and emotionally charged situations might be a real advantage. Still, he was tired of working his tail off to earn money to go to school. He had not found the meaning of life, and he hadn't had any fun either. Was he failing in life? He did not know, but he chose to take a turn in the road mostly because he felt like it, even though he was painfully aware that it was illogical.

Christopher was seriously in love. He had lost the battle. In the nine years he worked on his objective, he counted many successes and some major failures. He seemed no closer to knowing his purpose and the meaning of life than he did when he was twelve years old. He had learned a lot but not nearly enough. The paradoxes of life were overwhelming. He was making the first large but faltering steps to becoming a whole person, although he judged himself a failure for it. The integration of love and emotion into his life would be resisted and difficult, but it would be a struggle rich in learnings and paradoxes.

It would not be quite fair to leave others with the impression that the traveler, Christopher Daniel Bird, was totally into himself. He was extremely introspective for his age. Most of his peers considered him to be something of an intellectual introvert. This was known to and convenient for Christopher. There was no real need to have people know what went on inside his head. He did love sports and games. Just about any game that was a good challenge would provide temporary fascination and amusement for him. He attempted to figure games out. Card games and games of chance were fun but provided, in the long run, no value for skill. The rules of statistical probability could not be broken in the long run.

Even though Christopher thought of himself as being very pragmatic about the human condition, he was very much interested in the social and political issues of his time. While he was convinced that humanity disgusted him, he agonized about young men, his peers, dying in rice paddies and jungles in a far-away country. While war had a central place in human history, he thought it a senseless anachronism that had far outlived its usefulness as a method of problem solving. Nevertheless, he did not protest the war and he decided that if his lottery number was drawn, he would play out a chapter of his game in jungles and rice paddies. More troubling to Christopher was the fact that people were dying in the streets of his country to obtain rights and freedoms that were already guaranteed by the laws of the land. That anyone would think to convey more or less value on a human being because of race, creed, gender, or religion struck him as nothing more than ignorance, if not total stupidity. He participated coolly in dorm and student center debates on these subjects. Chris cared; he really did care about death, freedom, and rights, but he had no time. So Chris took up no passionate causes except for the game . . . his game . . . the search for meaning and purpose in life. He did not see that thinking these thoughts was a paradox or an oxymoron for him.

Chris did discuss, with finely disguised passion, the meaning of life and the soul . . . one's essence, other dimensions, death, and the possibility of existence after death. He prowled discussion groups in search of people who might share his passion for the game and his interest in other dimensions, particularly the dimension of essence. If there were others like him, he found it hard to know. It occurred to him that others were there, but they, like he, were protecting their inner thoughts. All of them were successful at protecting themselves from others knowing their interest in the game.

Somehow, Chris and his love made it through their senior year of college. Each succumbed to love in their own individual way and fought it, as they believed they needed to. Yet in the beginning, when they married, she did it for life and he for as long as the feeling lasted. As well as they thought they knew each other, in reality they had barely met. They could have never guessed at the joy, agony, and learning that would become their journey together.

With a mixed sense of joy and melancholy, Christopher journeyed on. There was joy at love. He had decided that it was fine and perhaps inevitable to love one person. (This was absolutely not a situation where one could logically go from a specific example to general application of a change.) He was unsure if it was or could be "until death do us part," but he thought it was worth a try. It really did feel wonderful. Another side effect was that the dream tunnel seemed to be reactivated, and, without really knowing why, he was again comfortable with it. Christopher was melancholy knowing that this was the end of a dream, his dream. *Ah yes, perhaps I can go to medical school next year.* But he knew that he would not. It was over.

He knew that something new was beginning. He was melancholy for the loss and wondered if he had failed. Although he intuitively knew that a new direction was appropriate, he had so ingrained the objective into himself that the change felt like failure.

It was a bittersweet time, a time of bitter endings and sweet beginnings. There was the melancholy of lost dreams and the joy and wonder of new ones, and the ecstasy of good sex with someone he was crazy in love with! Change, perhaps the ultimate paradox in three dimensions. Usually for something new to begin, something old has to end.

In later life and with some wisdom from the journey, Christopher would see the serious inconsistencies and paradoxes in his early life philosophies. In his youth, he most assuredly did not recognize these conflicts. In his quest for meaning, purpose, and ultimately perfection, he would certainly have fixed the problems, had he recognized them. It would not be much later in his journey that he would view these times with wonder that the person who lived this life had really been him.

CHAPTER 5

INTERMEZZO: THE FROGS

For what is a man profited, if he shall gain the whole world, and lose his own soul? Or what shall a man give in exchange for his soul?

Jesus in Matthew 16:26 (KJV)

Christopher and his new wife entered into the real working world together. They struggled in uncertain economic times to find jobs that were interesting, paid well, had good benefits, and were reasonably close to each other geographically. They changed jobs, towns, and cars. They talked endlessly about what to do with their lives now that they had changed course, she from being a serious symphonic musician to a music teacher and he from doctor to chemist. Perhaps in a couple of years they would renew one or both of the old dreams or develop new ones. For now, there was life to live. Jobs to go to, bills to pay, and fun to have, and they were in love with being in love. They hated fighting with each other, but they loved making up with each other!

To Christopher, this concept of fun was new in the sense that he had never expected to find it with a woman. She brought music, laughter, and color to his life that had never been there before. She listened to him ramble. After great sex, he would discuss life and existence after death, out-of-body experiences, and other dimensions until she fell asleep. He found this a little annoying, but she said that when he got "philosophical" it tired her out. He was concerned that he bored her, but she assured him that that was not the case. These discussions were fascinating but were so "heavy" that they tired her mind out. Often after, or even in the midst of, these ramblings, he slept and entered the dream tunnel, which just seemed like an extension of the conscious thoughts.

Christopher continued to have a great appetite for reading. He read everything from the classics to pulp. He read brilliant works as well as some brainless smut. History, philosophy, psychology, sociology, poetry, and music were all fascinating to him. He looked for the great answers, and when he tired of that or became frustrated he looked for entertainment. He found science fiction to be both entertaining and mentally stimulating. Just thinking of the possibilities was exciting. Still, the answers he sought were not seen.

He worked with a passion always striving to be the most efficient, the most accurate, the most precise, and simply the best. He cultivated neither friendship nor even good will among his fellow workers. After all, beyond the obligatory love of family, who really needs to love or even have care and concern for more than one person? From this, there was to be learning. The job became such a serious bore that Christopher could perform it with his brain shut off. In his boredom, Christopher rationalized that certain shortcuts were in order, because in his superiority he knew the outcome. Hence, he did not need to perform all of the steps. His fellow workers, whom he had belittled and ridiculed as dolts, lay in wait, and when he stumbled they kicked him ferociously. He was nearly fired. The pain of the faux pas was not in the near firing. He had seriously embarrassed himself because he had violated his own work ethic and personal values. The pain was great, and there were no dream-tunnel escapes. He forced himself to face his failure. He met with his boss and confessed to having screwed up and to the breaking of his own personal rules of behavior. He offered to be fired or to resign. His superior countered that Chris was his best analytical chemist and that this was a first offense. Christopher was not fired; however, there was a more serious consequence resulting from Christopher's arrogant behavior—his belittling of his fellow employees was disruptive in the workplace and they hated Chris. The boss said that six months of good performance and perfect getting along with his fellow employees would result in the removal of the letter of reprimand from his file. Christopher protested. "You mean I have to get along these idiots . . . ah, *people* . . . to get my record clean?"

It was indeed a difficult condition, but Christopher worked at being civil and respectful to his colleagues. His pain and embarrassment made him seem almost humble. After all, he couldn't really blame them for his mistake! He found that they eventually forgave him his arrogance in return for his respect. They weren't so bad, he guessed. Still, the lesson was a painful one. To have to admit to himself that he had failed at one of his cherished values was indeed painful. To have to learn to think about others' feelings and thoughts to pass a test was almost as painful. Consideration of others was not such a difficult skill to learn, he found. In fact, he found it almost natural after consciously practicing it a little while. He was a near total success except for a few moments of anger when his colleagues didn't pick up on new procedures as fast as he did. He did pass this test, as he did all tests, but there were serious repercussions for the rest of his life. It was a good lesson well learned. Although he would always have to work on his patience, a similar lapse in adherence to his personal values never again occurred.

This idea of working and playing well with others struck Christopher as odd. It was an oxymoron. Why do you have to like people to work with them? For a real person, an intelligent person, there is no need to like. There is only a need to decide and do! He discussed this with his love. She did not think it strange at all. In fact, she questioned what the heck he thought life was about. "Getting along with others is a basic skill you should have learned before kindergarten," she said to him. "You did go to school at four years old. I recall you bragging about it. How on Firterra have you managed to live all these years without realizing that you have to work and play well with others to be successful?" She continued. "I have noticed that you do not treat some of our friends with any respect sometimes, and you are even rude to me when I do or say something you do not like or agree with."

"But I love you," he blurted.

"Love is more than sex and liking each other. It's about respect and deep caring, and I am sick of your attitude!"

Christopher walked away in stunned silence.

Ignorant heartless bitch, he thought. *I give to her and her alone my love and share my most intimate inner thoughts, and now she wants to change me. I'm out of here.*

He went for a motorcycle ride and thought about the situation. He did not understand why she thought he should be such a wimp and be nice to everybody. After all, he was not mean; he just said what he thought. He went back home to pick up the discussion where it had been left. Meekly, he asked her for an explanation. She said simply that she was tired of being belittled and seeing others belittled by him. That he probably didn't mean to, and since he now knew that it pissed her off, she was sure he wouldn't do it anymore. He did not understand. If he had understood, it would still not have been an easy or immediate transformation from the habits and behaviors he had acquired and even cultivated and nurtured. How could he comprehend the concept of consideration of others? It had always seemed such a contradiction and so unimportant that he had never given it any thought. This debate between them and Christopher's behavior modification would last for years. In fact, his became a lifelong effort for Christopher, and the transformation would never really be complete, although the change would be immense.

It was not long before Christopher found the practice of analytical chemistry tedious and set about looking for a new career or at least a new job. In the course of changing jobs, his employer required that he take a series of complex and comprehensive psychological profiles accompanied by a consultation with a clinical psychologist at the option of either the employee or the psychologist. Christopher was curious about the test results beyond the written analysis he received but did not schedule an appointment. Psychology was not a very exact science, and besides he did not need a shrink to tell him that he did not know what was going on in life. He knew that already. However, the psychologist did schedule an appointment with Chris.

It was with great uncertainty that Chris greeted the psychologist, an older man in his late forties with graying hair, glasses, a gracious smile, and a calm, intellectual demeanor that put Christopher somewhat at his ease. The psychologist confessed that he had scheduled the meeting not because there was a problem, but because he had seen some interesting results in Chris's tests and wanted to discuss them with him. The psychologist said he thought he could be helpful.

Crap, thought Chris, *one of my little eccentricities is showing.*

The psychologist started the discussion by rambling on about having a couple of colleagues in graduate school who had attended the small university that Chris had attended. After a few compliments about the quality of faculty and students at that university, the shrink moved on to the important subject at hand and Christopher was in rapt attention. "You may have noticed," the psychologist proceeded, "that your written report described you as being very creative. That, in fact, was a severe understatement. Your scores were really off our charts for creativity. The fact that you have a degree in chemistry but are looking for a new career suggests to me that you should look at a field where your talents and creativity can be used to the best advantage."

"Really," Chris responded, "what does that mean? I've never really thought of myself as either talented or creative. I don't do art, and I am a musical disaster. My wife is an accomplished musician, but I can't even sing. What kind of talent or creativity could I possibly have?"

The psychologist smiled and steepled his hands and began a patient and kindly dissertation on the kinds of creativity that were a part of the makeup of humankind. The kind psychologist explained that there were talents in many fields. There were, for example, psychologists with abilities to help people who went beyond mere academic learning. They include talent and intuition. In fact, one might be a talented chemist but certain things in Christopher's test answers led the doctor believe that Chris had stronger and more valuable talents other than learning and applying technical skills to problems.

They discussed other facets of Chris's life: college courses of interest, sports, music, and in particular his reading. Chris was surprised at how comfortable he felt discussing these things with a complete stranger. Perhaps the guy really did know him. It was truly amazing how that test had gotten inside his head. The discussion ended with no real conclusions on what creativity meant for Chris, but the psychologist urged him to keep an open mind to all sorts of opportunities for personal growth and development that might present themselves to him.

Chris confessed to himself that he would really like to have some talent. He knew he was smart, but inside his head he did not think that being smart was as great as it had somehow looked to him at age twelve. He thought enviously of his wife's talent to make and teach other people to make music. He felt somewhat worthless and frustrated that all of his efforts and learning had not translated into anything of great value except a decent job. He did not think that he was any closer to the great secrets of life or his purpose than he had been at twelve.

Chris believed intuitively that there was something in this discussion of creativity for him. There was supporting evidence for the truth in the analytical conclusion of his creativity because of the precision and accuracy of the way he was described by the rest of the analysis. Still, he did not know what it meant to him. His complete being, clear to his very essence, called out for answers.

If he did have an idea what his talent was, it would not be so easy to change his life now. In the years since college, he had married the love of his life, and they had given birth to two healthy, lively, and active children. Christopher's solemn oath that his children would not grow up poor was as fresh in his mind as if it had been made yesterday. He was committed to this promise. That promise did not make him a great father. It did, however, make him a committed one. He had expanded his love horizon to include his children. After all, they were so cute and bright, and they were his. He could not just change his life now, could he? This was not a good time for change. He left the psychologist's office in a deeply thoughtful state of mind.

When Christopher arrived at home, he was tired from thinking. He took a nap and slipped into the dream tunnel. When he awakened, he penned a poem about essence and soul and their connection to existence. He enjoyed the verses of poetry that had recently been occurring to him as expressions of his feelings and state of mind. Although his poetry was extremely personal and private, he was subjectively impressed at the emotion and passion expressed in the verses he had penned. No link was apparent to Chris among the verses of poetry, the meaning of the word creativity, and the person Christopher Daniel Bird. Although he knew himself well enough to know that the passion in the verse came from deep within his soul, it was, and had always been, disguised and suppressed so that it seemed, even to him, to be disconnected from his identity.

Christopher's work life was progressing, although the rate of progression was not what he wished it to be. While he was being promoted steadily based on his hard work and performance, there were those around him who seemed to just cruise by him without pausing to look at him as they passed. He had heard a rumor that eight of his colleagues were predestined by senior management to be the senior management of the future. These eight were known affectionately, sarcastically, angrily, respectfully, humorously, and somewhat enviously as the seven princes and a princess. Chris had always dismissed the rumors as ludicrous and silly. This was America! There was not royalty or classes or preordained for success. So why would senior management be disposed to choose certain people over others as winners when the race was just beginning?

Shortly after the initial mental denials, Christopher smiled as he admitted that America was not a classless society. It was indeed possible to be more socially mobile in this society than in many others. With that myth disposed of, Chris took a long, hard look at the career progression of the princes and princess and compared them to his and others he considered like him. He had to admit that the *frogs*, as he referred to them, because of their ability to jump wide organizational chasms that others found impossible to traverse, were jumping ahead of nearly all competitors. Some other bright competitors forged skillful and powerful political alliances that fueled their careers, some with and some without any observable performance or achievement.

It became clear to Chris that in order to stimulate his career, more education was needed. In fact, a graduate degree might fill in that vacuum in his life left by not going to med school. He was embarrassed to admit to himself that, although he had avoided business classes and economics all of his life, because they were inexact sciences, he did not completely understand the economics that he been reading recently. After all, much of the population thinks that the world turns on money.

The pursuit of a master's degree in business administration filled many needs for Christopher. It filled the need for achievement left vacant by not going to medical school. It filled a need to learn, and he pursued the learning with almost lustful passion as if he had found the purpose and meaning for life. It explained the economics that he had previously read but did not understand. It provided a sound basis for his management of his personnel and family finances. Finally, it was another credential for career advancement.

The pursuit of the degree became the new dream. Christopher completed the program in near record time. He learned accounting, marketing, economics, finance, and management. He was not substantially differentiated from his fellow students. He spared no effort. Summer classes. Homework was completed while watching college football on Saturdays and the NFL on Sundays. Homework was done while watching movies and cartoons with the kids.

There were a few additional learnings that came as a definite bonus to Christopher.

After he had completed about one-third of the classes in the program, Christopher whined (to himself, because who else would really care since this was not something that he had to do?) that he was working his butt off, but his grades were mostly B's. Not great for grad school. Problem defined. Chris did a case study: situation analysis, problems and opportunities, and a solution recommendation were to follow. The situation was that he had violated *the rule of the expectation of the syllabus*. He had been on the reckless pursuit of learning without giving proper respect to the conformity lessons of academia. He was paying the price. The problem was conforming in order to exercise the opportunity for the better grades. This was the classic conflict of objectives known to force decisions based on the opportunity cost. Chris was older and wiser now than he had been in undergraduate school. He recommended, to himself, trying for one semester a rigorous following of *the rule of the expectation of the syllabus.* He followed the recommendation as prescribed. He was rewarded with the grades, as expected. Further analysis revealed to him that this was an easier course to follow. It wasn't really hard to figure out what professors wanted and that they really were in love their own answers. The medicine did not taste or feel great in retrospect at the taking, but the resulting A grades felt good.

The opportunity cost, Christopher thought, *could this be that old nemesis, the paradox, the contradiction? No, of course not. This was a sophisticated case of somewhat conflicting objectives.* It amused him and suited his purpose to submit to *the rule of the expectation of the syllabus.*

In a course on the social responsibility of business, the professor was so obviously brilliant and learned that Chris, following *the rule of the expectation of the syllabus,* was as quiet as a mouse in class. The course was tough. No easy A. He was not about to get into a verbal mind game with someone so vastly superior. He was actually intellectually intimidated to silence. Nevertheless, he had an opportunity to express himself in a paper that had a very open-ended outline in the syllabus. Chris researched and outlined his paper with all the diligence of a student who knew the grading would be thorough and exacting. The paper was written and rewritten, and Chris hated redoing anything. The paper was handed in per the due date, and the fateful day came for the return of the graded paper. It was with actual fear and trembling that he awaited the return of his paper. As it turned out, the return of his paper came last, and the professor said, "Christopher Daniel Bird, where are you and why are you silent in my class?"

Christopher's stomach turned and his knees trembled as he raised his hand and softly answered, "I don't understand the question."

The professor replied with a smile, "This is the most passionate and best articulated paper I have seen in any of my classes at this level.

Congratulations! Please express yourself in class, and I will see you in my office at the break."

Christopher was stunned, elated, astonished, and apprehensive at the same time. At the break, Christopher honestly confessed to being intellectually intimidated by the professor's obviously great learning. The professor smiled and said, "Well, you have no reason to be intimidated. You have a fine mind. Use it and speak up in class. Perhaps, when you are seventy-two, you will be honored by someone with a fine young mind complimenting your learning. You may go."

Now the irony was this: Chris did not think the paper extraordinary, but he treasured the high praise. In spite of his diligent efforts and exemplary paper, he did not get an A in that class. It was one of those paradoxes. He was pleased with his effort and the result, even though it was not the reward he had originally expected. *Perhaps*, he thought, *this was one of those experiences that was its own reward.*

Near the end of the MBA program, there was a pregraduation seminar class of cases that required students to integrate all that they had learned in solving complex, real-business problems. Each student's grade was determined, in equal increments, by class participation in the debate of the solutions, individually written case study papers, and a real-business consultation project. Near the end of the semester, to his surprise, Chris was again singled out. This time specifically for a paper on a case related to personnel management as well as the class discussion. The subject of the lauding was intuition and ethics. Christopher's intuition and his willingness to apply his personal ethics in the workplace, rather than applying an easier solution, were praised. "Furthermore," the professor lectured his class, "we shouldn't have to teach you ethics. You should have learned them at your church or synagogue, as well as at home. Finally, when analysis and numbers fail to suggest a solution to a problem, trust your intuition if you have any. Mr. Bird has a mega dose. Trust it, Mr. Bird, and use it wisely. It is a true gift."

Christopher wondered, *What good are these gifts and talents if I can't figure out how to use them for some benefit?*

Finally, he learned in several classes Maslow's Hierarchical Theory of Motivation. It made sense. The observable evidence of life supported it. It is so obvious that we all need food, water, sleep, and sex before we can move on to the next levels and think about safety, environment, ambiance, and luxury, not to mention self-actualization. He adopted the theory as a fact of life, and it became his theory of the why and when of purpose in life, moving and growing on the journey to eventual self-actualization.

Work hard, attain each level of the hierarchy, maintain what has been achieved, and move on to the next level. The drives to fulfill love and esteem needs were difficult to achieve and seemed impossible to sustain.

No matter, Christopher concluded to himself. *Someday, when I am older or even old, I will become self-actualized. If I am fortunate and have worked hard enough at life, I might even become a little wise.*

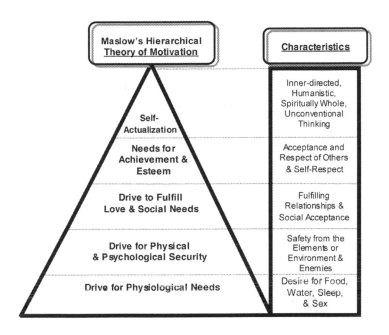

Christopher graduated with a master's degree in business administration. For a while, a very short while, he thought that he had filled in one of the gaping holes in his life. He had hoped that this would be a springboard for his career. It may have helped—he was never really sure. He did not apply the workplace variation of *the rule of the expectation of the syllabus*. He was not politically correct. He didn't strive to answer his superiors' questions with their answers. He did work and play very well with others and, in fact, had many friends in the workplace. He was considered a valued associate by the vast majority of his immediate superiors, peers, and subordinates. He continued to think that he was paid to be creative and say the truth as he saw it.

Christopher had a fine mind and a fine education. He had read the finest works in literature, philosophy, and poetry. He loved music: rock 'n roll, country, jazz, opera, and classical. He had seen the finest plays by Shakespeare, Williams, Euripides, and Weber. Yet his life was shaped by the simplest of philosophies: work is good, work is fun, and always work hard. Christopher was a true believer in the hard work ethic. He believed that if one really put out, then good things would happen. One would receive promotions, move up in one's organization, and make plenty of money. This philosophy and underlying assumptions seemed to work and be true for over twenty years.

Then the strangest thing happened. For the first time in his career, after being promised a promotion if his organization achieved 60 percent of certain objectives, both his department and his promotion vanished unceremoniously in a reorganization, even though they had achieved 100 percent of their objective. The explanations were vague and pregnant with corporate intrigue and double-talk. To add insult to injury, the idiots—the three vice presidents who delivered the message—asked him how he felt about the situation three times. Twice he replied he was fine and that this was not the worst thing that had ever happened to him. Although Christopher knew intuitively, that it was not the worst thing, it did at that moment feel like it was. Finally, he answered that he was not about to tell them how he felt. They probably could not handle it.

Christopher himself delivered the message of his and their demise to his team and then left the office for the day, seething with rage at the lies and nearly brokenhearted with disappointment that he had seriously misunderstood the system. He had not lost his job. He had lost all faith in the system. Christopher made one of those rare sacred promises to himself. He would never really trust the corporate world again, and he would figure out what happened.

The pain and grief that followed were comparable to losing a parent, spouse, or child, only in some ways worse. The death and corruption were both internal and external. The lies and betrayal were external, but the broken fundamental beliefs and values were internal and the pain of the unanaesthetized surgery was brutal and excruciating. Work would never be quite the same again.

Actually, this event did not come as a total shock to Christopher. Prior to the fateful event, it occurred to Christopher that if he did receive this promotion it would probably divert him from his highest and real purpose. He struggled with the terrible conflict in his soul. He wanted both to get the promotion as well as have the time to write. After slipping into the dream tunnel and coming to grips with the fact that one objective was truly higher than the other, he surrendered to the slipstream. As Christopher approached the point at which the message would be delivered to him, he knew deep within his soul that this promotion would not be. This prior knowledge did nothing to either dull the pain or mute the anger. It was an experiential paradox. Christopher, in his wrath, felt a sort of entrapment in his destiny. He questioned, Job-like, if the Creator had become a puppeteer playing the strings of powerless humanity.

Although he knew how to maintain a facade of relative normalcy, Christopher entered a state of paranoia. He vacillated between berating himself for being too dumb to figure out what was going on and fury at being screwed over and lied to. Christopher swung like a pendulum between pain and anger. When the pain subsided, rage took possession of his mind, and the heat of the rage and the power of the pain began to change him to his very essence. He would be remade from the most fundamental tenets of his soul, like the phoenix, transformed, but he did not know that yet. It was a time of death and new life. One dream died giving birth to another.

Following the anguish of being cheated out of a promotion that he had earned and expected, Christopher felt it was time to do some serious introspection and come to grips with the state of his life.

First, he felt he must determine if he was in the midst of a situation or if he had a problem. He was not truly unhappy. He was very dissatisfied. There had to be more to life than this: go to work, pay the bills, go on vacation, and around again. On a macro scale, this was just a circuitous, spiraling, downward path to death. A not so merry-go-down. Christopher had been through significant tests and difficult times and changes. He thought, *This is stupid. Certainly the frogs worked endless hours, or at least they spent many hours at work. But what did they ever accomplish? In the competition among them for the very top spot, a couple had moved to other companies. It's funny: the dumb ones left to go on to greater success than the smart ones. Clearly, I am as smart and as well educated as they are. So it's not about being smart. I have executed every assignment and project given me very well. It is an undeniable and inevitable conclusion that the game is not about accomplishments! Much that is published of business and careers then is a lie! What then is it about? It has always been said it's not what you do or know but who you know etc., etc., etc. That is a really stupid way to run an organization! I am really ignorant. I have totally wasted my time. This job means nothing in the grand scheme of things.*

Christopher was seriously depressed. He was despondent, lethargic, and without appetite for food or life. Although he had gone through a few bouts of what he called melancholia, he had never been one to be depressed for any length of time. He did get melancholy when he thought he had done something that he judged really stupid. He had gone through many stages of transformation to become a nearly complete human being. He had learned the value of love, loving, and being loved, respect and self-respect, giving and receiving. He was a well-thought-of husband, father, citizen, and employee.

He understood well that organizational synergy in any group—political, civic, religious, or corporate—came from the whole organization being greater than the sum of its individual parts. He also knew that each individual had great intrinsic value in spirit, in ability, and as a whole person. *So what*, he thought, *or is there a seed in this event from which to grow some meaning? What has no lasting value to me is emerging as well as a vague outline of what does have meaning.*

The depression lasted for several days. He did not think that he was journeying on. He took time off work to sit in a chair, listen to music, and wrestle with this, his dragon. Sometimes, he walked or jogged and wrestled with his thoughts. The dragon did not back away. Finally, Christopher decided that he had to deal with this situation or problem, and time was a-wasting. He sat down to do a standard case study analysis: situation analysis, problems and opportunities, and recommendations. As a result of Christopher's contemplation of his situation, he wrote a poem to explain the situation to himself. Amid the metaphor, simile, and rhyme, he looked the "Dragon" in the eye and began to be free.

The poet's conclusions were several. *The situation is that substantial changes are occurring in my life. I can act or react. The first is my choice and is distinctly offensive and active. The latter is passive, defensive, perhaps denial, and is not my style! I have set my own course in this company/career/job. This is where I am. It has been a journey. I have acquired learnings, experiences, and relationships to be appreciated and treasured. It is both better and worse than other people's company/career/job. It is mine. It is a part of my journey. The frogs really do not matter at all. This may be their game or test, but it is not mine. This job is something I do, but it is not who or what I am. I am choosing for this not to be my identity.*

Christopher's thinking continued. *Oh, no. I have been true to myself, but I have lost the game, or have I? I think that I have entered into one of those beatitude paradoxes. I must find the meaning in this. It is definitely time to begin to journey on. Life is not just a game, nor is it about whoever has the most toys winning! It's not about position, title, money, or possessions. So what is it about then? In fact, life is really not about that which can be seen and measured empirically and compared to other things like it. What we are is not necessarily related to what we do and produce in the physical sense.*

It was a time of change. It was neither the beginning nor the end of change. It was the end of the beginning. It was the benchmark place that marked Christopher's embrace of a purpose higher than could be explained in three dimensions. It was time for Christopher to set himself free. It was a time to enter into and surrender himself to the cosmic traveler's slipstream, whatever that is or might be. So he faced with joy a new pursuit. Chris gave himself permission to move beyond what he could conceive of in three dimensions and to commit himself to the slipstream to find and accomplish his purpose. It would take meditation, thought, and work to journey on. Christopher had learned that some events in the journey seemed to happen serendipitously while others seemed like a journey on their own.

CHAPTER 6

OPUS: THE SITUATION—CONFUSION AND MYSTERIOUS GUIDANCE

A look, square in the eye of the dragon, had vanquished the depression and fear. As Christopher washed the car, he realized that the dragon would return if he did not get a grip on himself and figure out what really mattered in life, and then do it. Gone forever the dragon was not! It felt good to work. Somewhere, he had read that hard work was good for the soul. His experience was that manual labor, jogging, or bicycling had a remarkable effect on his state of mind and spirit. As he worked on cleaning the car thoroughly, he began to carefully dissect who he was, what he was, how he had become what he was, who he appeared to be, who he really was, and what he really needed to become. The trouble with all this thinking was that it was full of irony and paradoxes. Nevertheless, for reasons that were not quite clear to him, he felt for the first time in his life that he could grapple with all the contradictions and make some sense of them. It felt good. He felt good. This too was paradox. On the one hand, he felt defeated, a piece of corporate filet mignon thrown in the corporate grinder with all the other cuts and ground up, ground down, beat up, and beat down but not submissive and certainly not beaten. He also noted that his was just a company. It was like many others: neither better nor worse. Really, seriously, this life journey is not about a company, an organization, or frogs. There is something much deeper and richer.

Sometimes, our biggest asset can be our biggest weakness, Christopher thought. *How long have I known that truth? Yet I continue to beat my head against the wall. I am no quitter. I am smart. I have what it takes. I can and will succeed. Wrong definition of success! Ahhh . . . I think I am getting the message: wrong road, pause and take a deep breath. Think! Go a different way! My head is bloody but unbowed.*

In fact, he really felt free for the first time in many years. The corporate machine had finally helped him realize a very basic truth. In a fashion, this was somewhat similar to that of a twelve-year-old boy he had known well years ago. His analysis was that he had a job and not a career. Frogs had careers. He was not one of the great corporate athletes, he was not particularly charismatic, nor was he one of the beautiful people who floated through life. Although he did seem to have a certain esoteric charm to a certain group of friends and acquaintances, his most remarkable trait was that he was bright and had the ability to integrate the things he had learned academically and experientially and apply them easily and quickly to problem solving. His solutions were usually a great success but simple, reliable, and unspectacular. He was not a great explainer of how he got to the solution. His presentation preference was this: there is the problem; here is the solution. Although he was considered to be one of the best with statistics and financial analysis, a problem solver, many of his solutions came to him intuitively. An explanation of the process of the derivation of the solution would have been difficult if not impossible for him. For this, he sometimes was accused of being secretive or even obstinate. Christopher thought of this as an amusing paradox.

Among the people he believed were interesting, he was regarded as being smart and a great colleague to have on the team when focusing on any serious problem. He did have a biting, sarcastic sense of humor that made it sometimes difficult (especially for superiors who thought that he thought business was just a game, if not a cosmic joke) to know if and when he was serious. He realized that he never had taken business as seriously as frogs did. He had always known that it was a game, a means at best, never an end. *I could never be a frog. Fine. What happens in the video game* Frogger? *Squish, trying to get to the other side of the road. Was it reality or just a parody of life?*

Christopher Daniel Bird smiled to himself as he observed that he had become, in some ways, exactly what he had intended to at age twelve. He was respected for being smart and, of course, a very objective problem solver. The scientific method played out.

So what? Do I value this? The resounding answer is no, not really. What I really value about my reputation is that I have a broad perspective and can integrate my learnings to meaningful solutions that, while not glitzy, have value.

It seemed that when Christopher explained his solutions people sometimes instantly knew that and, of course, he was obviously correct. The paradox was that the solutions he proposed were so obvious to him, yet no else proposed them. Christopher decided to store this thought away. It seemed to have some great significance for him. The bottom line of this little thought process was that the corporation had set him free. There had been years of exchange of value—sometimes equal, sometimes unequal. Christopher realized that he had left value (some would say money) on the table. His judgment of his own behavior was pragmatic and harsh, and the dragon peeked momentarily from its exile.

Okay, fine. Except for my substantial ego, I am undamaged. I am free of the delusion that the value I have left on the table is an investment in a career. I have made a charitable contribution to the company far above the equal exchange of value, but, as for me, I am free or at least in the process of becoming free. Therefore, the company and I will have an equal exchange of value while I work at understanding where I need to go and what I need to do to have a life that fulfills my real purpose. Really, it is worth the charitable contribution to know the truth and to be able to be free. The charitable contribution paradox is that it was a good investment. It is now time to move on!

The car was thoroughly cleaned inside and out, but the thoughts still flowed. It was time for a run, and run he did. But there would be far more analysis and questions and answers than one jog or one car wash could handle. So it was that the next leg of the journey began, appropriately, with the ironic paradox of the bitter disappointment that became freedom. With some fear and much joyful anticipation, it began.

Christopher had always loved William Ernest Henley's melancholy poem "Invictus." It declares the freedom of the human spirit and champions self-determination. The celebration of being unconquerable thrilled him. "Invictus" had fueled the fire in Christopher's internal boiler many times as he had used it for self-motivation to escape the martyrdom of his life as a poor farm boy trying to make it in life. Now Christopher smiled at his own self-pity and reveled in the fact that "Invictus" was now no longer shaded darkly by the gloom of a struggle to survive in the darkness of life but was rather brilliant in the light of the quest to find the meaning of freedom, of spirit, and of truth. He thought that *invictus humanus spiratus* sounded like a mass for the triumph of humankind!

While running, biking, and doing manual labor, Christopher thought his thoughts, asked his questions, and posed his answers. Conclusions began to reveal themselves, and Christopher continued to be amazed at the many times he had encountered good guidance but had not recognized or valued it. He had wandered in the labyrinth of the paradoxes of life. He also questioned whether all the guidance he had missed was intended to be seen later as a collage rather than each bit or byte separately. Another contradiction? He decided not to feel guilty or beat himself up for the signs that he had missed but simply be committed to understanding the collage now while finding his purpose and life's meaning.

Some conclusions emerged. He did not value his work accomplishments as anything that really contributed in any significant way to the overall good and growth of mankind. *My life has been equivalent to three grains of sand being tossed about the bottom of the mighty Mississippi River. I can do better than that! What I have done of value is love a family and a few friends. We have two not perfect but beautiful and wonderful children. I was far from the perfect or ideal father, but I did love and showed them that love, and they have never been poor. We have a son nearly through college and a daughter about to start. Yes, yes indeed, I have kept my promise. Although I promised myself that they would not be poor and succeeded, love was and is clearly the most important gift.* He stated all of this in his mind without a sliver of doubt. To bring closure to the solemn promises, he asserted to himself that he had kept them all but one: the most important one. He had not yet made a difference. In this rumination, he also concluded that the pursuit of that purpose alone would have either accomplished all the others or they would have become unimportant.

So, here I am. I am not twelve years old anymore. I have lived in the huge shadow cast by that child-man. It has taken me twenty-five years to unlearn the things that I overlearned and overtaught myself in about five years. I am nearly fully reintegrated. I am ready for my purpose. Yes, I relish knowing that I wanted to be smart and respected for it. I also know now that I have become that dream, and that by itself is an empty, tasteless shell. I treasure the knowledge that my children have grown up with some affluence, a rich mix of experiences, culture, and travel. They have never been poor. This promise will be completely fulfilled when our daughter graduates from college. Yet I treasure more the fact that I love and gave them love, and it is known and reciprocated by them. He smiled in amusement, amazement, and great pleasure at the thoughts of his children.

Christopher's theory of child rearing was a simple one that created its own vexing and ironic contradictions. The theory and practice were to teach children values, teach them how to think, love them, encourage them to be inner-directed individuals, and let them answer their own questions. It was not that he had no dreams for their development and success; rather, it was because no matter what he read or studied or who he asked, he had no idea how to motivate them or what really motivated people in general to any specific goals and achievements. He could not really explain his inner drive to figure out his purpose and the meaning of life. What was that perpetual bur in his saddle? The Christopher method of child rearing was influenced by, and principally implemented by, their mother. (Chris, in spite of love, had little patience with children.) This was imperfect, but it was simply the best they could come up with. The result of successful implementation of this method was, and is, assertive, confident, inner-directed, responsible, and sometimes argumentative children, adolescents, and adults. These individuals can be really annoying if you are their confident and learned parent wishing to shed your knowledge upon them. They tend not to be extremely receptive and can even be downright rude by stating their own views that they *know* are right and that you know are substantially different from your own. One can only laugh at the beauty in this contradiction and irony. The outcome is that they become the embodiment of exactly what you hoped and dreamed for, just not exactly and specifically the way you may have dreamed it.

Christopher continued his work on understanding the issues of his life: where he was in his journey, his problem, his case, and his situation. His thoughts meandered about the spectrum of his life until he focused on a more disciplined approach to this, his life and most important case study. The simple method of problem solving that he often used would serve him well again.

First, he worked on understanding himself. He subscribed to, as he described it, the Ayn Rand theory of individualism or selfishness. One must first understand and be true to oneself specifically before anything of any great value can be accomplished and before any real contributions of merit can be made to the human race in general. *So who am I? Paradoxically, and notwithstanding my pursuit of knowledge, I have thought of myself for many years as a simple farm boy just trying to make it in life. What I am is anything but simple. I have evolved in a complex process light years away from that bright but unbelievably ignorant and naive boy. I am still in the learning process.*

He realized that externals drove much of the process, although he had often prided himself on his control of his life. A life was a journey and not a controlled experiment. The things and events that he had forced or controlled had frequently been disasters or at best difficult to overcome. The learning of the scientific method and applying it to all of life had taken years to unlearn so that he could learn to trust his intuition again.

Christopher realized a few things about love. Falling in love had been an extreme, out-of-control experience, but it had come from within. Love had never been and could not be forced. It had come from within. True love, real love, was given freely and unconditionally. It would be a long learning process to remove conditions from the giving and accepting. There were many times that humans perverted love into what it is not. Often the trading on the illusion of love made people behave irrationally, crazy. Much evil had been done in the name of love. In the name of love and god, there were holy wars and killing over different worship protocols and dogma. There had been irrational killing over different views of God and worship. In the name of love of race and ethnic pride, there had been ethnic cleansings, genocide, and holocausts, and the insanity seemed to linger in humanity. It seemed like such an obvious oxymoron. It was so incongruous. In its pure form, love is perfect. At that moment in time, Chris was jolted by a phrase that he had heard and read many times but until now had been empty words: *Perfect love casts out fear.* Of course, he thought, and the power of the thought actually caused him to shudder physically.

There were certain things that Christopher had ground around in his mind for years and had studied and made many empirical observations of. He thought, *There is definitely good and evil. There is definitely a light and darkness, God and Satan respectively. The light and the darkness are a part of this life test-gift-journey. Many times evil, that which is bad for us, is packaged and marketed to look like something wonderful. Likewise, that which is good for us seems difficult, onerous, and objectionable. In three dimensions, the time illusion causes us to focus on now, this minute. The concept of putting off present pleasure for future happiness requires a longer-term, essentially other dimensional or spiritual, view of life.*

During Christopher's continued self-evaluation, he realized that one's perspective on life was hugely influenced by one's experience. That each individual's view of current and future events is relative to his or her perspective of life. Simple empirical observation of this relative perspective idea was the one that was so often discussed when witnesses to a particular event gave different interpretations of what had happened. Christopher thought of how many times his view of how much money was a lot had changed. When he was a child, adults had seemed huge. As an adolescent, a week or month had seemed like a long time. Now, as he was neither old nor any longer young, weeks and months were a short time. Geographic concepts were even more striking: a two-hundred-foot-high hill was a significant mountain until you had been enthralled by the beauty and majesty of peaks over fifteen thousand feet tall. To a young farm boy, a city of one hundred thousand people seemed as big as it got. To a well-traveled adult, a village of a hundred thousand was barely worth noting, unless it was a vacation spot. So, he concluded, *What is real and true to each of us is, to a large extent, influenced by our past experiences.*

Yet all is not relative, he thought. *There is much the human family shares. We all, with rare exceptions, know what is round, square, cylindrical, blue, or yellow; the sun rises in the east; it is cold at the North Pole; it is hot at the equator; water is H_2O; and other physical facts. We all bleed. Stuff happens without our choice. We all die.*

Do we all wonder about the hereafter? Christopher's conclusion was that we share many things; the commonality contributes to order and effective communication. We have many differences; the differences and diversity in humankind and our environments contribute to the variety and richness of our interactions and individual journeys. There is also much that we, humankind, do not know and either have different views on or do not care about. Christopher concluded, *My Big Deal is understanding the meaning of life and my purpose in it. I suspect most of us wonder about it, but most either do not take time to dwell on, do not care, or are afraid to ask, and a few seem to know.* He shuddered as he contemplated the possibility that he was the only one who was too stupid to see it. He shook the thought off because he just didn't think he was that dumb. *I am sure that I am not alone in this quest. I know that there is much written of it and that what I have read and experienced leads me to believe that there is both commonality and individuality in the meaning and purpose. There should be some deep paradox in the answers,* Chris thought with a grin.

Finally, Chris concluded there had been something curiously consistent but mysterious about the clues in his life and relationships. He was perceived by some to have some talent and perhaps a gift. Perhaps it was that intuition thing? It was usually those same people who told him he needed to do something to make a difference. There was even that time his mother-in-law told him specifically that one person could make a difference and that she thought there was something he should do to make a difference.

He remembered his favorite teacher saying so long ago: "You have a special gift; you need to figure it out."

Pretty vague and speculative information to go out and do anything with if it were merely serendipity. He knew that there was danger here, the risk of looking stupid. Risk of appearing to be what, the fool? On the other hand, the paradox: what could be dumber than pursuing an objective like a jackass following a carrot on the end of a stick that is tied to one's head? The corporate illusion has been that carrot. That puts that risk into sharp perspective. Christopher's thoughts continued. *Maybe it is all influenced by my experience? I have already been the jackass, and I know it. I no longer need to travel the path of a twelve-year-old. The words "When I was a child, I spoke as child; now that I have become an adult, I must speak as adult" come to mind. I am beyond that shadow. Therefore, I can risk appearing to be the fool. Mere serendipity is not my conclusion on these mysterious inputs. I feel neither talented nor gifted, but my intuition, which I know but do not feel, is strong. It tells me to journey on this new road.*

With some anxiety but no distress, Christopher Daniel Bird decided, *Although my mind and my very soul cry out for the answers now, I must journey on until we find each other!*

CHAPTER 7

THE CRESCENDO: PROBLEMS
AND OPPORTUNITIES

For God hath not given us the spirit of fear; but of power,
and of love, and of a sound mind.

2 Timothy 1:7 (KJV)

Christopher sat quietly on his patio and regarded this new freedom with the wonder of adoring parents taking the first loving look at their newborn offspring. He realized that it was great gift and awesome responsibility. There was an opportunity and a problem! The beauty of the gift was that he could be who he really was. Say what he really wanted to. Do what he wanted to do. Most importantly, he could now give himself permission to do what he needed to do. The responsibility was to do the right thing! Somewhere in the back of his mind was the barely conscious thought that a rampage of freedom misused and abused could do an enormous amount of evil. *So, a* thoughtful Christopher mused, *I must be careful to do what is right for me, and if I keep in touch with my essence, ask for help, and put aside my ego and preconceived ideas, I will discover my mission, my purpose, and the meaning of my life.*

As he perused the possibilities, Christopher bowed his head, asked for help on his journey, and thought. *I guess that I have always known the truth. That a large part of who I am, and indeed part of the basic nature all of humankind, is spiritual. It is difficult to piece together the evidence of that truth only on the basis of empirically observable facts. It is rather a part of our common intuition. It is odd that so many people who give animals credit for having instincts are unwilling to give themselves and all humankind credit for having higher instincts, greater than animals. A conscience, a still small voice that can only arise from the depths of the soul, is denied. It is the very essential common core of all humanity. In the entire search for knowledge, and what I really believe about morality and destiny, I have never really doubted the existence of my other dimensional essence! I have spent a lot of time and energy creating and maintaining a facade that separates my physical three-dimensional self from my essence. The result has been wasted energy and emptiness. I have not allowed myself to be complete. I have lacked wholeness of the integration of the mind, body, and soul.*

I wonder how many others think and feel as I do? Now I need to dream the dream and know my purpose. The dream? What is my dream? Christopher chuckled as he thought, *Or rather, what have I dreamed? The dream tunnel is really the place where I have researched and incubated most of my many esoteric thoughts on knowledge, morality, destiny, and essence. It is there that I seem to know and be comfortable with my own purpose. It seems now that if I surrender to it and embrace it, it will indeed become my destiny and give meaning to and be the meaning of my life. It almost sounds foolish to me when I think it. No matter. I have played the jackass, so I can risk being myself.*

There has been that nagging sense that I should write down some of these thoughts and stories that come to me or that I dream or think or whatever. It sounds kind of silly, but perhaps, maybe, just maybe, my dreams are not just serendipitous but are part of the macro pattern of the collage of my life. What stories have I been told and what thoughts and insights do I have that anyone would possibly want to hear or read about?

The question was a large one to which Christopher had no answer. He did feel the need to record what he felt and thought. *Perhaps I can just to be an instrument?* He paused for a time and asked for help before he journeyed on.

Equilibrium: The MultiQuations of Life

> *In the Beginning God created the heaven and the earth . . .*
> *and God blessed the man and the woman, and said unto*
> *them, Be fruitful and multiply, and replenish the earth,*
> *and subdue it . . . and God saw everything that he had*
> *made and behold, it was very good.*
> **Genesis 1:1, 28, and 31 (KJV)**

Christopher lived in a time when it seemed that humankind had seriously altered the condition of, if not the actual character of, the physical environment of Firterra. Irresponsible and selfish mining, farming, and land development techniques had raped the land. The forests had been plundered. The rain forests that remained were being destroyed daily before the inhabitants and stewards of the planet really even knew what they were, what lived there, and what secrets and solutions were held there for some of the problems plaguing humankind. The waters were poisoned every minute by thoughtless and ignorant contamination. The habitats of many of the thousands of species with which they shared their home were being destroyed or altered beyond the survival limits. Humankind was pooping in its own bed.

Christopher wrote passionately of his concerns. "Hello, hello out there! Does anybody care or do all of you want to sleep and swim in your own feces? How could we really ever expect to meet and survive with species that are higher than we, in this dimension or any other? What if they treated us as we treat those species under our care, not to mention the way we treat each other?"

Firterra was essentially a closed system that received energy from the outside but at the same time operated in a larger way within a huge macro system, a solar system, a galaxy, and a universe. It was also true that the Firterra was in an automated evolutionary process as a part of its universe. It was undergoing change that was sometimes slow and subtle as in climatic change. And other times were rapid and violent as in earthquakes and volcanic eruptions.

Christopher's audience was not easily convinced. "Yes," they said. "So what? Almost everybody knows this stuff. Why talk about it if you cannot propose any realistic solutions?"

Christopher, who was not one to be easily deterred from delivering his thoughts, replied, "But we do have the answers. The basic instructions that came with our home say that we are to replenish it first and subdue it after that. The instructions do not say that if we rape, pillage, and plunder our world that it will be kind to us and heal and replenish itself. Our science knows well the theories and observation of chemical equilibrium. Simply, chemical reactions within a controlled system tend to reach a state of equilibrium at the lowest energy state and remain so until energy and/or reactant are added, products are removed, or temperature or pressure changes are imposed. We cannot clear-cut a forest or burn a rain forest (i.e., destroy habitat) and expect species that are both aesthetically and physically important to us to survive. In equilibrium terms, destroying a forest is removing the product so thoroughly and completely that the equilibrium state shifts. The reactants are exhausted and equilibrium is radically altered or destroyed. If we are thorough enough at this process, we could possibly alter climatic conditions or even destroy our automatic source of clean, breathable oxygen."

Christopher continued with his thoughts to his fellow Firterrans. "We can only harvest so many tons of fish, by specific species, from the lakes, rivers, and oceans, without destroying our supply. Likewise, we can only disturb so many miles of spawning rivers with hydroelectric dams before we lose the ability and choice to harvest and eat the delicate salmon and other species that have thrived there since the dawn of time. Try running the financial analysis on five hundred miles of salmon-spawning grounds, a financial perpetuity, against a hydroelectric dam with capital investment and maintenance costs. What you will find is that, if you were charged the full cost for what it has actually cost all of us, the electricity would be more expensive than any of us would be willing to pay, both implicitly and explicitly. It has often been found that the first or easiest solution for hard problems is not the best one."

The instructions and the evidence of equilibrium on Firterra seemed quite clear to Chris: They could take all that nature could provide while still replenishing herself. If they needed or wanted more than that, they needed to find ways of replenishing her and themselves.

Christopher further expressed concern for the health of his home and fellow inhabitants of Firterra. "It seems that nature has been pretty forgiving and the balance of equilibrium broad enough to tolerate most of humankind's subduing since we have been successful at being fruitful and multiplying. The time for sane replenishment is here. It is really past time.

"The basic instructions suggest to me that we have the ingenuity and resources to figure out the many equations that relate to life and to act appropriately. There are thousands of individual components in the *MultiQuations* of life, but they are not all rocket science. We must learn to live within the broad bounds of the many equilibria in our three dimensions. The poisons that we can create, we can and must neutralize and destroy after their productive use and before they contaminate our environment. The quality of the home that we all have and contribute to for ourselves, our children, grandchildren, and generations beyond depend on us. It is only the development of our love for ourselves, our environment, and our love and respect for our Creator that will motivate us to do the right things."

The Illusory Peace

*Glory to God in the highest, and on earth, peace and good
will toward humankind*

Luke 2:14 (KJV)

In Christopher's time on Firterra, peace threatened to show up
but never made it. Peace had begun to bloom and freedom had
begun to ring around the world in places that had not seen them
for generations with the fall of an ugly wall that had imprisoned
millions and failing totalitarian regimes. It wasn't long before the ugly
stepsisters of the Cold War—ignorance, poverty, spiritual vacuum, and
terrorism—lifted their ugly heads to replace the Cold War! The rise
of conflicts around Firterra after the demise of the Cold War was a
kick in the gut to peace-loving people all over Firterra. Christopher
sadly observed that the absence of great wars between nations did not
mean that all was well on Firterra and that his world was at peace.

Christopher observed the human struggles for peace and freedom
on Firterra in his time and place in the continuum. He studied the rise
and fall of peace and freedom at different times and places throughout
Firterra.

He noticed that that in some places, the revolutionary concept of
freedom was in its infancy, entrepreneurship bloomed, crime and black
markets flourished at first, and millions whined. Whined? Why would
millions whine? It is the ubiquitous paradox that stalks life in three
dimensions. With freedom, there is responsibility. No more planned
economy. Everyone is responsible for making quality products and
providing quality service for each other. Without competitive quality
products and services, economies fail and people lose their jobs.
People who lived their entire lives being told what to do and what
to believe enjoyed the ecstasy of being free individuals. They also
learned the anxiety brought on by choices and not having someone
else, that rotten government for example, to blame for what happens.
The concept that we are the government is a cold shower of reality
after the hot initial passion of newfound freedom.

In some places, freedom was taken for granted. Crime rose. There seemed to be a need for social programs to teach people the basics of life, hygiene, values, and, perhaps most important, respect for themselves. Christopher knew that where there was ignorance and poverty, there would not be peace. Ignorance was not bliss! Poverty created desperation and fear. There were people who would compromise freedom for a perceived sense of security. Special interest groups would have bans placed on certain things that they believed were responsible for the demise of social values and the rise of this or that vice.

Certain groups of people wanted to have pornography and other works not to their liking banned, but they were highly incensed if anyone should think of banning or limiting the promotion of one of their particular beliefs or pieces of literature. Christopher believed that this was sometimes a well-intentioned but misguided objective. It was founded on the premise that people can be sheltered from evil and temptation. The truth was that the beings on Firterra could not be sheltered from evil and temptation. They could be taught right from wrong and the power of the light and the slipstream to help in resisting temptation and evil. Morality could not be legislated. Unfortunately, society could not elevate individual members to right and the light by lawmaking. Individuals lifted to the light through love would not be deceived by the temptations of evil.

Christopher came to understand that freedom's bounds were defined by free individuals not exercising each of their own freedoms to the detriment of any of the rest of the individuals in society. Freedom cut both ways and was blind to the particular preferences of any one individual while protecting the rights of all.

Peace, freedom, a fundamental respect for life on Firterra, and a responsibility for life and each other were inexorably connected. They were all contingent upon each other. They were not mutually exclusive.

It seemed to Christopher that one of the greatest tragedies of modern Firterra was the destruction of unborn life. He was baffled that peopled exercised the freedom to fornicate and copulate without taking responsibility for the opportunity to propagate. He understood from basic biology class that the process of the propagation of life begins at the moment two reproductive cells unite and the zygote begins to divide and multiply. At the moment of beginning propagation, freedom has been forfeited in favor of responsibility and the respect for life. To Christopher, the question was about life and responsibility. It was not about a woman's freedom over her body. It seemed that if men and women are responsible and competent enough to, after a reproductive act, take a life in cold blood, then should they not have even more responsibility to be considerate of each other and the potential consequences before the act? He concluded that the means of birth control were both known and available! The simplest and most effective of all methods of contraception known is responsible self-control. Responsibility is the solution. When an unwise act or decision of any kind is completed, responsibility continues, and it is not abrogated. This responsibility includes the commission of simple acts of compassion.

Christopher considered the maxims *Put off present pleasure for future happiness* and *Love is patient* to be fundamental. He also concluded that the misconception that sex is love was one of the greatest illusions of existence in three dimensions.

Abortion was a serious societal question that speaks to the very foundation of freedom. The liberty taken to abort life and responsibility undoubtedly deprived Firterra of some very gifted individuals destined to make contributions to their advancement in philosophy, the sciences, and the arts and deprived society of some great humanitarians. Sadly, the empirical evidence was that those aborting motherhood and aborting fatherhood had not really erased responsibility, but most of them suffered varying degrees of psychological pain and damage to themselves as a result of their own acts.

Exercised freedom and aborted responsibility does not equal peace, either individually or collectively. Christopher did not condemn the freedoms but rather anguished at their momentary enjoyment or exercise without a longer-term view of the resulting consequences. When Christopher was tempted to enjoy the hedonistic pleasures of Firterra, he reminded himself to beware of the illusion that self-discipline is the enemy of joy and pleasure, rather that responsibility and self-discipline are part of love and are the catalysts for lasting joy and peace.

Christopher became painfully aware that peace, world peace, is not a dream that becomes reality because of a treaty among nations or a change of type of government and/or the governing laws. It is the result of the millions and billions of individual pieces—each of us—being at peace. The whole is equal to the sum of its parts in geometry. In organizations and society, the whole is intended to be greater than the sum of its parts due to the human synergy of focused energy and teamwork. Peace requires a bold new geometry; each piece, free and responsible, each piece at peace. It is easier to identify the enemies of peace as ideologies, governments, or religions other than our own, or human organizations, than to identify and attribute responsibility for the contribution each individual makes toward peace.

Christopher came to the realization that the concept of peace based on the contingent tenets of freedom, responsibility, and spiritual health would never be accepted by all Firterrans. It might not even be adopted by a simple majority of them. It is too simple. There are too many illusions that collaborate to make it seem impossible and silly. Nevertheless, the message needed to be written down and the words said. So he did. He reasoned that it was a small thing to be considered foolish by some in order to make a difference in the lives of many or even a few. *What if, perchance, just a few individuals change? Maybe that will make a huge difference.*

Christopher believed passionately that there would be no peace in his world until there was an awareness of the basic essence of humankind and a focus on spiritual healing rather than a total focus on temporal existence in three dimensions. He had learned that it was objective of the dark side to keep beings in three-dimensional existence infatuated in things temporal at the expense of the consideration of eternal existence and the consequences of such deliberations.

Love at Midnight: The Beginning of Understanding

*And now I show you the most excellent way . . . If I
have . . . all knowledge . . . but have not love, I am
nothing. If I give all I possess to the poor . . . but have not
love, I gain nothing.*

*Love is patient, love is kind. It does not envy, it does not
boast, it is not proud . . . Love never fails . . . when
perfection comes, the imperfect disappears . . . now these
three remain: faith, hope and love. The greatest of these
is love.*

1 Corinthians 13 (KJV)

The Bird kids were growing up and begging for a pet. Christopher
and his wife discussed what to do. Dogs are great pets and children
do learn responsibility by caring for them. So they decided that a dog
would become part of the family.

It was a small, black, fur ball. She was a mutt, regardless of the
thoroughbred parentage: a thoroughbred golden retriever mother
and thoroughbred black Labrador father. A twenty-five-dollar pet.
The first night she cried constantly except when the children took
turns cuddling her. Chris, as father, built a large doghouse for the
mutt. In the first months, she was banned from inside the house. She
was a crazy, wild, and undisciplined puppy. She was black and her
name was Midnight. As the months passed and the children bugged
their parents, Midnight was allowed in the house for short periods
and only under the strictest of conditions. She began to walk with all
of them and jog with Chris.

This dog seemed particularly eager to please and be with her
family. She would always greet them with a joyful bark, a jump
straight up in the air, a large furry wagging black tail, and, if they
got near her, she would rub up against them and make the most
affectionate doggy sounds. However, she did not do what she was
told. So it was decided that dog obedience school was needed and she
was enrolled. It occurred to Christopher that since the children were

ten and thirteen years old, this dog, Midnight, was going to be his in the long run, since she would likely be alive long after the kids had left home. So Chris and Midnight went to school.

In school, Chris was struck by the sweet and humorous truth that in dog obedience school he was learning as much as or more than the mutt. They both learned a lot, and a curious bond was created between them. Although she seemed to prefer to play with the kids, she would frequently look at him when the rest of the family gave some direction to her. This *secret* bond was annoying to the rest of the family but was a special joy and amusement to Chris. Weekends were not complete unless she and Chris had gone jogging together at least once.

They moved into a new house before the yard was sodded and landscaped. The dog needed more than just a doghouse to stay out of the mud and mess, so Christopher built her a small deck. As her behavior continued to improve, she became a more frequent visitor to the house, and her stays were longer. Her behavior was impeccable. She never made a doggy mess, and she seldom chewed on anything she wasn't supposed to, but she sometimes liked to lick things.

After three or four years, their friend became fat and lethargic. Her beautiful, long, black coat became dingy reddish brown. She dieted to no avail. She got fatter and no longer jogged. Long walks were difficult. Her personality was in the pits. Midnight looked sad. Then, after some investigation, she was found to have a thyroid condition that could be treated. The medication might have a side effect, but it would no doubt improve her energy level, her coat, and return her to the outgoing dog she had once been. No expense was spared, and she reluctantly took her medication. In a few weeks, she lost weight and her high energy returned. In a couple of months, she was happily jogging again. In a few more months, her coat returned to the shiny black that her family had all come to love.

As the years rolled by, Midnight continued to jog with Chris and added frequent jogs with her adoptive mother and friend to her exercise duties. The oldest child, the son, left for college but was always greeted with a bark, a straight-up jump, and a wet kiss upon his return visits. Later the daughter also left for college. She too would always be greeted with a bark, a straight-up jump, and a wet kiss upon returning home. Midnight loved to be in the house with the Birds, and they loved it too. It seemed that the house was too quiet with both children gone. Chris and his wife expected and looked forward to many more years of companionship with their beloved and faithful friend.

One day Chris returned home from work and his loyal friend merely looked out of her doghouse at him. He called her, and she slowly and reluctantly came to his side. No bark, no jump, and no excited wagging tail. He gave her a little hug, and she followed him slowly into the house. Chris and his wife discussed Midnight's behavior and, although they were both concerned, they suspected that she was spitting out her medication again, when they weren't looking. They both thought she looked sad. They watched her for a few days, and the lethargy seemed to come and go. Mrs. Bird took her to the vet just to make sure she was all right. But the tragic news was that their long-time friend and loyal companion was thought to have terminal cancer. She had lost fifteen pounds, which they had not noticed because of her long, luxurious coat. The vet was running tests to confirm her diagnosis but had strongly recommended that they put the dog to sleep. She was in great pain and might live a few more days or even weeks because of her great love for her masters. She might even rally her strength and appear normal sometimes. Christopher went into denial. This could not be true! She was too young. She had not even been with them ten years! She could live much longer!

Unfortunately, the tests showed conclusively that their beloved companion was terminally and untreatably ill. It did not seem fair. It was just two weeks until Thanksgiving and the kids would be home. Chris thought they could give her medication and then they could all say their good-byes after the holidays. No, his wife told him tearfully, Midnight was in great pain and might not even live that long. If she did, they would have put her through awful pain for their own benefit. Christopher sat down by the Midnight and took her in his arms and began to sob uncontrollably. As he sobbed and rocked, he felt the beating heart of his beautiful dog Midnight. Her black coat glistened in the light, and she looked at Christopher knowingly. She weakly licked the tears from his face, which only caused him to sob harder. Christopher's mind said he was a fool and that this was just a dog . . . but his heart knew, as Midnight did, that they had for many years shared a special love. She was his favorite running pal. They had shared many secrets, and yet there were no secrets between them. They had loved completely without pretense or limits.

Of course the kids, Midnight's family, had to be called and told that she was going to die. Each of them broke down and cried and sobbed and talked to their doggy on the phone to say good-bye. Chris had to go out of town the night before Midnight passed on. He hugged her and told her how much he loved her and how much her family loved her, but that they couldn't ask her to keep on living in pain and they were all going to miss her. As she looked knowingly at him, hot, bitter tears of grief ran down his cheeks, and he bid one of my best friends and greatest loves good-bye.

Midnight died peacefully in the loving arms of one of her best friends, who was also her adoptive mother.

On Thanksgiving Day, Midnight's family cried and sobbed and grieved for their loss, and they each talked about how this dog, just a mutt, had been one of their best friends ever. To the son, her brother, she had been a friend who helped him survive when the family moved and he felt lonely and friendless. To the daughter, her sister, she had been a best friend when her brother had left home for college and she was lonely. To the mother, her adoptive mother, she had been friend and companion when the house was lonely and too quiet, empty of children. To Christopher, her adoptive daddy, she was a constant friend that was always glad to see him, was eager to exercise him, and always loved him.

At the end of Midnight's journey with them, they celebrated the gift of companionship and, most of all, unconditional love that she had given each of them. Through their tears and smiles, they were all truly amazed at the wondrous gift that their beautiful Midnight had given them and pondered the lesson it was for their lives individually and together.

CHAPTER 8

FORTISSIMO: CONCLUSIONS/
RECOMMENDATIONS—UNDERSTANDING

Do not worry about your life, what you will eat or drink;
or about your body . . . is not life more important than
food . . . Who of you by worrying can add a single hour
to his (or her) life? . . . But seek first his kingdom and his
righteousness, and all these things will be given you as well.
Therefore do not worry about tomorrow, for tomorrow will
worry about itself. Each day has enough trouble of its own.
Matthew 6:25-34 (NIV)

There was a moment at which Christopher sensed that although he
was not old, he was no longer young. In that moment, many thoughts
and emotions washed over him, and he was nearly drowned by their
enormity. He felt mortal, very finite, and even small. Insecurity,
personified as the dragon, surfaced from the deep as a huge, obscured
behemoth with fiery eyes. Just as Chris began to immerse himself in
accomplishing his purpose and the writings, the dragon chided him
with the reminder that he had not yet accomplished his purpose.
The dragon challenged that this was another of those meaningless
pursuits that he had given himself to, although none with a passion as
complete as this—and who will really read your book anyway?

Christopher, his learnings not being wasted, turned and looked the dragon in the eye. In that moment, he began to feel refreshingly alive as never before. The look at the dragon was, in fact, inspiring. Chris realized that he and his purpose were a work in progress. He paused, asked for help, and entered the tunnel on his way to emerging. After falling out of tunnel, Christopher settled into the cosmic slipstream and journeyed on.

> *Where your treasure is, there will your heart be also.*
> **Luke 12:34 (KJV)**

As Christopher advanced from his meditations, he was aware that many changes had occurred in both his three-dimensional self and his essence. Things that he had always cared about and thought to be of the utmost importance were seen to have little meaning. Things, activities, and material possessions that he had valued most in his life were seen to be of such a limited and transient nature as to be unworthy of the time and energy investment that they had been accorded. His purpose became his highest value, and he surrendered himself to it. Indeed, he gave himself up to it and found freedom that he had never known before. *What if these new writings are for my own edification only and are just a part of my development? No matter. It is still work that I need to do, and I can enjoy it and use it to reinforce the lessons I have learned and the wisdom I have experienced. My journey will be better for it, and, no doubt, the Papoo part of me will relax and my soul will be at ease when it is finished.*

One day during the writing, Chris had to take a business trip. It was a cloudy gloomy day in the city before departure. Once in the air for a while, Christopher observed the shadow of the clouds surrounded by sunshine on the ground below. In the shadow of the cloudy day, it was indeed cloudy, but from a higher perspective the gloom was surrounded by sunshine. This seemed to Christopher that this was another simple lesson in the value of taking a look at any situation from a variety of perspectives before pontificating about it. Christopher wondered as a result of this observation and the constant change and learnings that came from increased experiences and a variety of perspectives on life, of what he was certain?

Christopher contemplated this question and realized that for him it could not remain rhetorical. In order to continue his growth, he needed to define and articulate his worldview. As he deliberated on these things, his learnings and beliefs crystallized in his mind.

Life is gift to be enjoyed. Love, unearned and unconditional, is the greatest gift of life. It is the giving and receiving of love that makes life work the way it was intended. This love, both from your fellow beings and your Creator, is not something that can be understood by trying to understand. Rather, it can be understood only by surrendering one's self to it such that one is totally immersed in it. Only then does the freedom of understanding come. Love is too simple and difficult to understand without being dipped in it. A cherry sitting on a chocolate bar is not a chocolate-covered cherry.

Life is filled with many humorous and sometimes vexing paradoxes. One of them is that youth is a gift in which many of the facets of life seem to be enjoyed the most. Youth is a time in which most people think that they must figure out life and set out on a course for success and happiness. The illusions of youth are many and include both a sense of immortality and, on the occasions in which we understand our lack of wisdom, a corresponding feeling of hopelessness. Rare are the individuals who enter the cosmic slipstream in youth and comprehend that there is wisdom in the surrender of ego in order to have and become everything. This is perhaps the most challenging maze of all the paradoxes. It is a truth well concealed by many illusions, although it stands simply and in plain view of all.

Christopher's continued with his thoughts. *It is a special and powerful truth that the Creator's son came to Firterra and died for me, not just for humanity collectively but for me individually, in order to provide a means of connection to the cosmic slipstream. It is the most beautiful and powerful paradox that surrender to the slipstream is freedom instead of slavery. Rather, it is slavery that results from exercising the freedom to go it alone, pursuing the blind alley and illusions of the three dimensions. It is the simple truth of the beatitude paradoxes.*

He continued with that train of thought and concluded from his experience that it is only in the slipstream that love is perfected. Centered in the slipstream, there is a sense of completeness and comfort with one's self and the journey of life. In the slipstream, the giving and receiving of love have a color and shape. There is a wholeness that is not found in any other state in life. In this process of developing wholeness, insecurities and fears begin to vanish. The colors of life take on a vividness not previously perceived or experienced. There is freedom of mind and soul in the cosmic slipstream not found in any other psychological or spiritual circumstance. The bond to the material three-dimensional world is diminished as spiritual development progresses.

Christopher thought it sad that it is not until old age that humans, when life is stripped of many of the illusions of three dimensions, discover the richness of their spiritual nature and surrender themselves totally to the cosmic slipstream. Unfortunately, many realize that they could have enjoyed the journey more if they had been in the slipstream at an earlier point in our journey.

In his contemplations, he returned to his childhood. *I nearly entered the cosmic slipstream at five years old. Instead, I took the path of a virtual forty-year trek in the wilderness. Long after I discovered my mission, I denied it because I was afraid to give up myself, my ego. Fear is a trick of the dark side. Perfect love does expel fear. Fear is the shadow of the cloud. Love is the sunshine surrounding the shadow. As we grow older and have invested time and energy in that which has no meaning, we sometimes begin to see, by the process of elimination, what does have meaning.*

Christopher had long been aware of the paradoxes and ironies of life. Things like one's biggest strength can be, and often are, one's biggest weakness. In his own case, Christopher was intimately aware that his strength of self-reliance had many times prevented him from even thinking of seeking help or consultation in life, let alone asking for help. And yet he also knew that in some of those times that he had asked for help, cosmic and spiritual, or in the more conventional three-dimensional sense the help he had received was beyond his expectations. It had sometimes taken years to see the wisdom of both the simple and the cosmic answers. Many times the acquaintances he had asked for help acted as if it had been he who had helped them or eased a burden for them. He was certainly on a long journey from the twelve-year-old boy who envisioned life, his life in particular, as an unconnected island or perhaps even a singularity.

An introspective Christopher considered the many things that he had learned that were valuable but were either incomplete or led to wrong conclusions. Maslow's Hierarchical Theory of Motivation was one such learning. In the usual scheme of things, Maslow was right, but his thesis was incomplete, making the theory at the same time wrong. Christopher thought it was a rich paradox.

Some Rich Paradoxes

> *Man shall not live on bread alone.*
> **Luke 4:4 (NIV)**

When Christopher was first introduced to Maslow's hierarchy, he knew it was right. The idea rang so true and the flow of the logic was so obviously valid that he accepted it as one of the fundamental explanations of human behavior. Most of the empirical evidence certainly supported this theory, although psychology did not really verify the exact order and relative importance of each. However, he wondered, *Can psychology prove anything really?*

In the process of successive and repetitive thought over the years since he had accepted the theory, he also began to question it. He struggled with the uncertainty of knowing what constituted graduation from one level to the next or at least knowing when one should be focusing on the next level. Once one is beyond the satisfaction of physiological needs, one discovered that other needs can scarcely be satisfied for more than short periods of time. Christopher found that some things were less desirable to him than others. His needs for esteem far outweighed his particular needs for social acceptance. He began realize inherent conflicting needs. In fact, Christopher found that he had gloried in some of personal eccentricities permitted only limited development in some of the other tiers. These included, but were not limited to, a blatant unwillingness to be politically correct especially at the expense of honesty or truth. He never felt that he had enough money to be satisfied that he was financially secure. He had never been rich enough to pursue some of excesses of the rich and famous. However, given the drive to fill the emptiness and the opportunity, it is possible that he might have been no different from them. His attempts to be self-actualized on his own were unsuccessful. Reading the finest books and poetry, listening to the best music, viewing the fine and the historic relics of man and nature, combined with meditation, did not bring the peace he sought. Like the rest of humanity, he had to periodically revisit level one to sustain himself. Something about this idea of building on the basest drives of human nature appeared to be wrong or incomplete. There are many examples of human behavior returning to level one in desperate circumstances. Murder and cannibalism have been practiced to sustain life. In contradiction of the hierarchy, there were also many examples of humans making great sacrifices in challenging circumstances, such as during wars and persecution. People willingly sacrificed their lives for their beliefs or for loved ones. This is a stark contrast to the behavior that might be expected based on Maslow's theory.

Finally, in order to make the theory work for him, Christopher had to add to and modify it. First, he concluded that there must be balance and equilibrium between the levels, else the theory breaks down and it becomes increasingly harder to achieve the next level. To cope with this, Chris added arrows showing that there was an equilibrium that was potentially different and dynamic for each person as the conditions in life varied. This seemed to address most of his issues, except the many individuals who have given or endangered their lives for noble purpose: Gandhi, Joan of Arc, Jesus, the early Christian disciples, Mother Teresa, and many others came to mind. The behaviors and actions of individuals such as these suggested that they were fully self-actualized and that they were operating in a spiritual/psychological system where self-actualization had become the first tier, the basis, of life. The vast majority of all these individuals are clearly in touch with life and existence beyond the three dimensions. From this, Christopher concluded that in order to have a satisfying life with peace and balance, then Maslow's pyramid must be turned upside down and the pyramid must be pointed at and touch something more substantial than self.

Although Christopher was in a grand spiritual metamorphosis, it did not occur to him logically, at that moment in time, that Maslow's pyramid actually described two states of humanity. One had a focus inward and a state of spiritual emptiness and the most basic animal needs driving behavior and attitude. The other option was the pyramid in perfect balance on its point, the focus on essence and eternity, in contact with the Creator. The concept of a life with self-actualization and spirituality as the most fundamental driver appeared to Christopher while pondering the thought that "the present is the point at which time touches eternity," as written by C. S. Lewis. It was like a huge light had gone on in his mind. It was obvious that this must be the connection from the three dimensions to the other dimensions. This minute interconnection with infinity and essence, intuitively, without Einstein's math, explained his dreams and the tunnel. It is our soul that is our essence and its infiniteness that gives us this understanding.

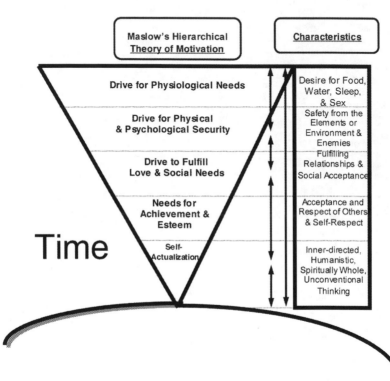

Maslow's Hierarchical
Theory of Motivation

Characteristics

Drive for Physiological Needs

Desire for Food,
Water, Sleep,
& Sex

**Drive for Physical
& Psychological Security**

Safety from the
Elements or
Environment &
Enemies

**Drive to Fulfill
Love & Social Needs**

Fulfilling
Relationships &
Social Acceptance

**Needs for
Achievement &
Esteem**

Acceptance and
Respect of Others
& Self-Respect

Self-
Actualization

Inner-directed,
Humanistic,
Spiritually Whole,
Unconventional
Thinking

Time

∞ / Eternity

Of course! Christopher thought. *Life is about the journey and the connection with infinity, God, and our soul. What makes life spectacular is the integration of everything and what is possible. It is not about what or how often I eat. It is not about how much I possess or where I live, where I vacation, what I read, or what music I listen to. If and when I become properly spiritually connected, I will become self-actualized and at peace with my life, my essence, and myself. All else in Maslow's marvelous pyramid follows. This is the connection to the cosmic slipstream of our journey.*

It was at that precise point that Christopher's soul touched God. As he meditated on this point, at this truth, his essence became one with the Creator and he was transformed. The priorities of life changed and the purpose became the slipstream.

Christopher realized that it is the connection to God that is the slipstream. It is the place where love can be perfected. It occurred to him that it was the lack of this remarkable connection and the fear left in the void that drove people to relentlessly commit themselves to compulsive behaviors. These compulsions—the relentless pursuit of power and wealth, neurosis, psychosis, and other afflictions, such as addictions to drugs, alcohol, and sex—were the result of a journey in the parched desert of the soul, devoid of spiritual water and nurture. Christopher had discovered the reason why many journeys built in Maslow's original hierarchy were withered, wasted, and miserable failures in spite of the appearance of having all that could possibly be needed to be happy and self-actualized. The journey, in order to achieve happiness and success, must be built on the fulfillment of our essence, not on base needs of the delusional three dimensions.

In Christopher's journey, there was a concept known as the "American dream." This was the belief that anything was possible in life and that all of humanity is entitled to life, liberty, and the pursuit of happiness. That those born into any circumstance or status can work hard and expect to succeed and achieve their dreams. That life is full of endless possibilities and constrained only by the taboos resulting from an incomplete understanding of the responsibilities of freedom. That an individual can have and be a part of family where love is given and received. That one can become self-actualized. Christopher had lived in times when the dream was espoused as very much a part of life and in cynical times when the dream was declared dead. While the mood in each of these times was obviously a contrast of optimism and pessimism, the dream never died in the hearts of mankind.

In reality, the dream is not particularly American. It is either dormant or growing in the heart of every man, woman, and child on Firterra. The dream immigrated to America with religious fanatics, political malcontents, economically disenfranchised, criminals, dreamers, and opportunists of every conceivable type and from every nation and tribe. Their diversity enriched the dream.

The pure dream is not a desire to rape, pillage, and plunder the land and destroy the environment so that one can be wealthy beyond all imagining. It is not to take advantage of the weakness, caused by illusions, of one's fellow human for one's own gain. The dream is one of happiness. If the dream is distorted to the pursuit of any compulsion, whether it is wealth and power or other, it is because the individual has mistakenly assumed that the ascent of the pyramid will lead to self-actualization and ultimately happiness. That is an erroneous assumption of titanic proportions. Humans have proven in countless journeys that the only thing that brings true happiness is the result of spiritual fulfillment. All other pursuits provide, at best, temporary satisfaction and ultimately only emptiness and frustration. The connection to God provides the only true peace and freedom in life.

Christopher thought with some embarrassment about all the years that he had read and been taught, without getting it, that perfect love casts out fear. He regretted the many years that he had listened without hearing or really understanding but smiled at the thought that even the mostly imperfect love that most of us give goes a long way toward making life a joy. Chris determined that since Papoo had taught him that life is not about regrets over the past, but about making the most of the present and of our learnings in the collage of lessons from the journey, he would journey on with joy.

Christopher's entry into the slipstream did not happen magically, nor did it make life particularly easier in a three-dimensional sense. It did make life more spiritually fulfilling and happier, but life was not all joy. The sailing was imperfect, for sometimes Christopher focused on his own three-dimensional course and did not pay attention to the telltale warning that the slipstream was changing. It was a process of changing and learning, a surrender of ego, a confident acceptance of some issues in life and essence and the passionate pursuit of some things and opposition to still others. The journey was imperfect as a result of Christopher's own imperfection. However, his intentions and motivations had glowing beauty. When he faltered off course, as a result of his own independent and self-reliant pursuits, he would recognize his error, pause, ask for help, and reenter the slipstream.

In his writings, Christopher theorized that humans in touch with their Creator and essence would no longer destroy their environment and their marvelous fellow inhabitants on Firterra. Christopher believed that there was work and a job for everyone and that in the cosmic slipstream all journeys are interwoven with infinite possibilities. No job is greater than another is. Furthermore, he believed in one of Solomon's most profound paradoxes concerning the pursuit of knowledge and wisdom, that with much wisdom comes much sorrow and with more knowledge more grief is added to life. To whom many gifts are given, much is and shall be expected from the mission and the journey. Some souls are blessed without a burning passion to do and/or find their mission, and simply doing and being what they are seems to be their mission. Others seem pulled toward destiny and are driven by an unseen force. Christopher accepted and pursued his mission with a passion.

The why of the need for writing had always been before him, but as usual was another paradox; it was almost too obvious to be seen. It was quite clear that all was not well on Firterra. There was persecution—ethnic, religious, and gender—occurring on a vast scale in many parts of Firterra. Where outright persecution did not occur, there was the frequent abuse of employees/workers, spouses, and children. Children were killing and were being killed by adults and each other. Rage and evil were on open display as murder and mayhem in every corner and niche of Firterra. In addition, the environment was still being ravaged with reckless abandon despite dire warnings from scientists and ethicists. Rain forests burned, toxic chemicals were dumped into the environment, and plants and animals were endangered or destroyed before they were understood.

Compounding this mess were those ubiquitous paradoxes. Consider the company that stressed customer satisfaction with no consideration for employees who were expected to produce this same satisfaction. Management geniuses and outrageously expensive consultants who could see no contradictions in the cutting and demanding more for less with little in the way of credible leadership. It was seldom said by any of the fashionable, expensive, and of course politically correct business gurus of the day that happy employees generally make high-quality products efficiently, which leads to economically produced, high-quality, and profitable products with high customer satisfaction. The more subtle signs of the emptiness and futility of journeys were the proliferation of seemingly inorganic disease, chronic and random psychological disorders, and suicides, which were the ultimate concession to failure and loss of hope throughout the human family.

Because a creation that exists in more than three dimensions cannot pull itself to the top of the pyramid by itself, it needs to be said that the paradigm of the pyramid must be turned upside down. The evidence has long been in. Maslow's theory, with a foundation in humanity's basest instincts, is a failure because it is incomplete. Maslow did explain half of what he observed.

"So," Christopher wrote with all the passion he could muster, "let us turn the pyramid upside down and slide into the cosmic slipstream of self-actualization that starts with God and love. It is obvious that it is a course of little risk; no other model or theory has worked for humanity. The proof can only be understood by making the connection to eternity. For those who demand proof, it is there. But it must be found by each individual."

Christopher continued with the robust certainty taught to him long ago by his teachers in the continuum of perfection. "I am sure that you have accepted many things on less evidence. Have you ever seen electricity? How many of you have ever seen your brain think or your heart beat? Yet these are accepted facts! Food is not tasted and provides no nutritional value if it is not eaten. Believe, and your life and pyramid will be positively turned upside down and you can happily journey on!"

CHAPTER 9

INTERLUDE AND FINALE: THE FINAL LESSON AND THE VOYAGE BACK

Christopher was on R & R, a break from traveling, to discuss the ideas presented in the book. It had been two years since the book was published. He had surrendered to the cosmic slipstream and embraced it. He had finally finished the book and, after a reasonable time, found an agent who became his good friend. They then found a publisher.

Christopher was renewing his spirit in the great western wilderness and engaging in stimulating conversation with his best friend, Reggie. Reg was well read, well traveled, brilliant, interesting, and conservative. He had not been consulted about the book but was among the first to read it. While Reg did not agree with all that Christopher wrote, he did understand it well and loved the ideas. He always said that it might have been better if Chris had presented some of his thoughts as hypotheses rather than firm facts. Christopher chuckled and replied that he believed them and his relationship to what was in the book was based on facts. It was simply his reality. Reg sometimes marveled that his friend Christopher was not totally mad. They were quite different and alike, and they enjoyed each other immensely because of both the similarities and the differences.

On a crisp and clear autumn day in the western mountains, Christopher and Reggie were hunting mountain sheep and the elusive mountain lion with cameras. Christopher sat patiently in his naturally camouflaged perch and smiled to himself at the changes in his own life.

The book had been well received by the public, and Christopher spent much of his time talking to people about the concepts and philosophy of the book. In addition, the book also received critical acclaim for its fresh thought on old problems and concepts and the creative story line. However as might be expected, there was a wide range of opinions on the writings and no middle ground. The paradox is that the very things that were lauded by some were poison to others.

One reviewer criticized the book as "fluff, soft, and emotional, soft answers to hard problems that needed solutions from the worlds of science, business, sociology, and psychology." Some reviewers said it was misleading to the public. The very idea that a personal relationship with the Creator and love for one's self, all creation and the Creator, could solve the problems humankind is encountering is preposterous. This novel was obviously written by an intellectually challenged, unsuccessful, and embittered person who did not have enough work to do. A few elitist editors of esteemed publications of science and academia sniffed with wounded professional pride that these writings were the ravings of a lunatic. One even gave the professional diagnosis: "All that dream stuff is serious hallucinating. This guy is either on drugs or is one strange dude!" Then there were the obvious declarations that Christopher was in no way qualified to make some of these statements because there was simply no proof. In spite of, or because of, the criticism, *The Upside-Down Triangle* sold well throughout the world.

Christopher sat in his hunting blind and pulled one of the caustic reviews from his pocket and reread it. He chuckled so heartily and audibly that he startled the bighorn sheep that were grazing and moving toward him. He regained control of himself and chortled quietly at the desperation of the reviewer's attack on *Triangle* and its author. The review stated that people with such delusions of connections to higher powers were often charismatic but their psychosis was still lethal to them and any who would follow their path. It was the part about charisma that he savored the most; obviously the reviewer did not know him. Simple, interesting, engaging, yes. But charismatic, no, he was not!

Then there were the critiques of various world religious leaders. They contradicted each other as one might expect. Some of the organized fundamental Christian church leaders accused Christopher of heretical and new age teaching. Where was his loyalty to the church, theology, formal worship, and church leaders? Furthermore, the concepts were just too new age. The self-proclaimed new age leaders said the philosophies and concepts of *Triangle* were too traditional and fundamental, and the liberal Christian churches agreed. Jews, Hindus, Moslems, environmentalists, Shintos, Confucians, atheists, and agnostics all agreed, for the first time ever, that these writings had some good concepts, but they were just too Christian. The Zens loved the paradoxes.

On Christopher's road trips and during interviews, he had been questioned about his critics and the possible validity of the criticism. At first he had been amused and a little hurt by the criticism and had refused to discuss it on the basis that people are entitled to their own opinions, and at least people were reading his book. However, after some questions by friends and acquaintances, he had decided to specifically reply to his critics but to neither argue nor debate them.

On his two most recent road trips, Christopher had joyously given his answers to the critics. "Yes, there is passion and emotion in my writings. Yes, it has softness. If it is fluff to you. I apologize for not properly communicating the message to you. Perhaps you would do us both a favor and reread it with an open mind and soul. Soft answers to hard problems, yes. None of the hard answers that have been offered up and tested are working in society. Misleading the public, no. Suggesting a different path and that God and love are more fulfilling than anything else, yes! Intellectually unchallenged, unsuccessful, and embittered, yes! Outside the slipstream, millions of pieces of evidence show that we are intellectually unchallenged, unsuccessful, and embittered, yes."

Christopher continued. "Furthermore, I have not been challenged intellectually in the corporate world, although patience and sanity were routinely put to the test. It is a waste of human capital not to listen with open minds to the many differing concepts and solutions that lurk in every nook and cranny of an organization, just waiting to be caught. We need a training program for senior management in all types of organizations, from churches to corporations to schools and universities, on listening and encouraging. Great, perhaps stunning, ideas are likely to come from employees, students, parishioners, volunteers, and constituents from all types of backgrounds. The mix and diversity of backgrounds and ideas is what truly creates synergy and makes the whole greater than the sum of its parts. If any organization is not experiencing synergy, if the whole is not greater than the sum of its parts, it is, to use a vastly overused word, *dysfunctional* and has no real reason for existence.

"Often politically correct management speaks about leadership, empowerment, and integrity. These are most often spoken when they are restricted or do not exist. This is a paradox that wants to be an illusion. When there is much public talk of empowerment and the great value the human capital and ideas in the organization, it is usually an indication that managers, who should be leaders, have some knowledge that there is unrest in the organization. They either do not want to change or have not a clue what to do. They call in expensive consultants and hold seminars in hopes that the unrest will be appeased and the problem will go away. Talking and listening to constituents is a freedom almost never exercised when it can be substituted with a two-inch-thick, multimillion-dollar consultant's study."

Christopher continued his passionate response to the learned and PC critics. "Real leadership hears and understands the many seemingly unconnected ideas and brings the ideas and people together as a master jigsaw puzzler. Leaders connect the dots. Managers conversely are the sheep dogs of humanity. Sheep dogs bark a lot and stick to the back end of the flock. It is difficult to lead the flock from the rear! Do you need more proof that common sense is truly uncommon?"

Christopher addressed with mild amusement the personal questions and comments made by some. "Dreams, hallucinations, psychosis or drugs? First, yes, dreams. You can have them, and I hope you do. We all have an essence that is other dimensional. Denial, as you know, does not change reality. Hallucinations and drugs? No! Psychosis . . . crazy? Maybe. Who knows? What is the standard for sanity, and what is the true measure for it?

"What proof is there of any of this? Well it's one of the paradoxes: there is proof, but I cannot prove it to you. The proof is in the cosmic slipstream of life and essence. You must find your own special proof. It really is a risky choice: sacrifice ego to have fulfillment and joy in life that is available no other way or retain ego and continue the search! You choose.

"Yes, I have experienced all of this on my journey. Have you, and are you? I wish that you would take the risk!"

In a careful and contemplative tone, Chris addressed the religious leaders and commentators. "I confess, yes, this really is Christian. It is my understanding of the core of what Christianity is meant to be. No, I do not think that my concepts favor any form of worship or dogma. I believe that a commitment to surrender self, ego, and living in the cosmic slipstream is the same no matter what theological constructs or mechanisms are used to explain it. Yes, that is what I believe and stand for. It has been said that 'you have to stand for something or you will fall for anything.' Do you need more proof of this than the simple observation of daily life on Firterra?

This is not a belief system against or at the expense of anyone. It is for anyone who wants to try it. It is a paradox. It is free, but it will cost you everything."

Christopher continued to journey and to write. Although he continued to have much success, he believed that he had never written anything more inspired and passionate than *Triangle* and his early poetry. He felt great satisfaction that he might have made a contribution to international cooperation in protection of all land and sea habitats and the ongoing development of exploration and equilibrium plans for each habitat before what remained was spoiled and squandered. Still, progress seemed slow, and he was growing older. Most of all, he was pleased to think that he may have been used as an instrument, a catalyst, in the development of many individual peaces.

In Christopher's eightieth year on Firterra, he developed a heaviness of soul and a sort of despondency that his journey was coming to a close and that he had not accomplished all that he wished to. Humankind was not progressing at a fast enough rate. In an effort to regain his usual energy and joy for life, an aging Christopher slipped into the dream tunnel and felt the long-familiar presence of his mentors: Gabriel and the Creator.

Christopher thought, *Oh, Creator where have you been? I need you so. With your inspiration, I have written elegantly of the Eternal Continuum of Perfection, and I have done my very best to live in the cosmic slipstream. Yet as I approach my imminent transformation, I find that I wish to continue to live in the three dimensions and that my work is not done. I am not ready for transformation, and I have not approached the perfection that I dreamed of. I have enjoyed life but faltered out of slipstream many times on this journey.*

The presence of the Creator answered, "Christopher, my beloved Papoo, you are right that the job is not done; however, your assignment is complete. It is up to others to continue the progress on Firterra. You have not achieved perfection during your journey, nor will you if you continue on. You have undergone a transition process that has developed the perfection of spirit that was a necessary learning for you to complete your mission. You have changed immensely since you first recognized your need to surrender your ego and become whole with Me in the slipstream. As you well know, your perfection is not complete in the three dimensions of Firterra. It is in the Eternal Continuum of Perfection where we become a perfected whole. Be at peace. The point at which you transform to the continuum is near."

Christopher awoke with a start and was surprised to find himself still on Firterra. In his thoughts, he found both excitement at his impending transformation and a small flavor of dread. *What if all that I have thought, written, and spoken of are the illusions and delusions of a mad man? What if, in the end, I have not carried out my mission well enough? What then?* He paused in his thoughts and asked for more help, as was his time-tested and honored habit, and then he journeyed on. He had embraced the slipstream and had done his best, and he knew, deep in his soul, that this was what was required of him.

Christopher enjoyed the next two years as he had not enjoyed any other part of his life. He loved and was loved by his wife, children, grandchildren, and many friends. Christopher, family, and friends engaged in lively debate about current books, theater, and emerging equilibrium plans. Life was pure joy except for the aches and pains of an aging body.

Christopher noticed that he had lost all sense of dread for the approaching transformation. He knew that his body was wasting away and that his vehicle for life in three dimensions would soon be gone.

It was a warm, sunny, spring day in the small mountain town on Firterra that was his home, and Christopher was walking his dog Angel. Christopher felt strangely energetic, and it seemed that he could almost feel a warmth in his bloodstream. The two walkers paused as Angel examined a scent. Christopher experienced an overwhelming sense of light and weightlessness. He nearly shook himself to walk on, but the peace of the light was so great that he lingered on to enjoy its warmth and journey on. At that instant, Christopher ceased to exist in three dimensions.

CHAPTER 10

HOME AT LAST

Christopher entered the tunnel and, unlike any previous dream, began to accelerate at what seemed like light speed. He seemed to be passing a mural of his life in three dimensions whenever he had been in the slipstream. It was wonderful, but the beauty was shattered for an instant as he beheld pure darkness. Papoo wondered where the record of his failings had gone. The journey continued at such a rapid pace that it seemed impossible to him that he could comprehend it or that he had ever been Christopher. As he perused the mural, he was awed to see the frequent presence of his friends Gabriel, Michael, Raphael, and Melchizedek, as well as the Creator, throughout the journey. He peered back to Firterra and saw Angel patiently sitting by an empty three-dimensional body.

Papoo arrived with a brilliant flash of light in the Eternal Continuum of Perfection. He was stunned at the beauty of the arrival area. The area looked brilliant white, accented with gold and silver. He took a long look around and was surprised to see his beloved teachers Gabriel, Raphael, Michael, and Melchizedek standing at the side of the Creator. There seemed to be thousands upon thousands of beings surrounding and basking in the dazzling light emanating from Creator. The angelic orchestra was playing, and the choir was singing a welcome-home anthem.

The powerful yet gentle voice of the Creator resonated. "Welcome home. You have completed your mission successfully. Please join me eternally in the Continuum of Perfection." Papoo was completely overcome with joy until the Creator asked, "Do you have any questions?"

This was the moment that Papoo had journeyed for. The first question that came to his consciousness was, "What happened to the record of my failings?" He gazed uneasily at his beaming teachers.

The Creator peered at him with a knowing look and replied simply, "There is no record of any failings. They were all forgiven. Do you have any other questions?"

At that point, Papoo could think of nothing more than how awed he was at the journey, how long he had pursued a dreadfully wrong path, and how often, even after he entered the slipstream, he had steered off course and had to ask for help to get back on course. But he had made it home. What was more amazing was the help had always been by him just waiting to be invited into the journey with him.

Papoo thanked the Creator for His love and support on the journey, and he said that he was surprised but could not think of any more questions. At that, the throng began joyous cheering and Papoo moved to the happy presence of his teachers and friends who had gathered to celebrate his homecoming.

Afterword

Magic is the willing suspension of disbelief.
Faith is the substance of things hoped for and the evidence
of things not seen.
Darkness is the absence of light.
Dreams are the stuff reality is made of!

It was with excitement, anticipation, and even some fear that I took on this project. In the beginning, my fear of failure and lack of substantial faith in my ability to do justice to the inspiration kept me in darkness. As I consciously worked on banishing my disbelief, my faith in my ability to record this story grew. With the growth of faith, I plunged into the full light of inspiration, and it brightened my journey. My passion for the project consumed me, and the story poured out onto paper.

It has all happened since I had that dream in Florida several years ago in which I promised some being named Papoo to write down a story that he, she, or whatever, *whoever*, would tell me.

I leave it to you, the reader, to decide: Is it a silly dream, an overactive imagination caused by too much contemplation of the mysteries of life and living, insanity? Or is it a valuable parable for today? I hope it has some value to you. It certainly has been a wonderful journey for me. I wish you well on your own journey. Love much.

RJC